ROSE'S LOCKET

TO Kelly + Corby

— Shannon Quist

ROSE'S LOCKET

SHANNON QUIST

NEW DEGREE PRESS

COPYRIGHT © 2020 SHANNON QUIST

ROSE'S LOCKET

ISBN

978-1-63676-630-0   *Paperback*

978-1-63676-256-2   *Kindle Ebook*

978-1-63676-241-8   *Digital Ebook*

For Emery.
Out of all the Roses in the world, you're my favorite.

MAP OF ZOPHREN

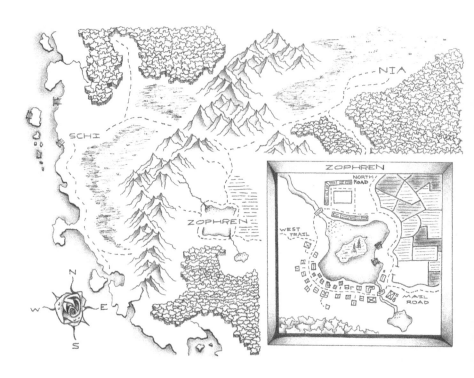

Artwork by Josephine Davis

ROSE'S FAMILY TREE

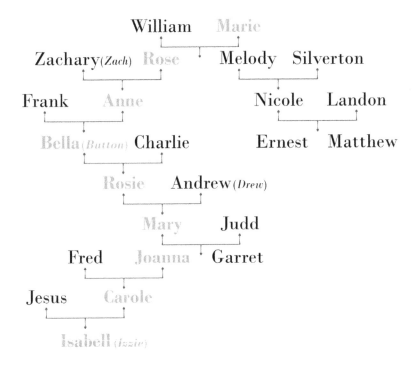

William — Marie

Zachary (*Zach*) — Rose — Melody — Silverton

Frank — Anne — Nicole — Landon

Bella (*Button*) — Charlie — Ernest — Matthew

Rosie — Andrew (*Drew*)

Mary — Judd

Fred — Joanna — Garret

Jesus — Carole

Isabell (*Izzie*)

CONTENTS

———

AUTHOR'S NOTE

———

I sat in the front seat of my mom's white suburban as she drove north on the loop on a still and bright morning. We were headed to my junior high for another day of school, and the radio was set, as always, to the local Christian radio station. But I'd spent my whole life listening to nothing but praise for God, and lately all I wanted to do was ask questions. The wrong questions, apparently.

As we drove in silence, I looked out the window and let myself fall inward. Gazing across flat empty fields, I was suddenly overwhelmed by an out-of-body jolt—my thoughts raced from slight annoyance at the radio to realizing my utter powerlessness over my life's direction.

How did I end up here? Why Earth? What was the point? Where would I go? I was adopted into this family, and suddenly that meant something different. It didn't feel special anymore; it felt dark, like I didn't belong. So, where *did* I belong?

I didn't have any answers to these questions, and I certainly didn't trust anyone enough to help me answer them. So, I held on tight to the sleeves of my oversized hoodie and did my best to swallow them down.

Just before this particularly vivid crisis, I learned that there was much more to my adoption story than my parents had ever told me. I had always known about being adopted at birth, but then stumbled upon documents containing more information than I was emotionally prepared to handle.

Later, when I was much older, I returned to that empty and helpless feeling inside of me and began to finally seek out answers about who I was, where I came from, and how I could find meaning in my life. During my divorce, I found a therapist who figured out how to handle me despite the rocky wall I'd spent years building around my heart. Early on, he told me that we would be talking about existentialism and handed me *Man's Search for Meaning* by Victor Frankl.[1]

"I don't want you to waste your time trying to find out who you are," my therapist said. "I want you to focus on creating who you want to be."

But creating identity and meaning aren't easy tasks. Studies show that adopted children struggle more with things like identity formation and a sense of belonging.[2] For most, this is caused by gaps in their stories. For us to navigate who we are and where we belong, we look in two places—our past and future. Scholars in cognitive narrative theory agree that our brains comprehend and empathize best when we're given information through stories, so if we look at life as a narrative, our individual lives are a single chapter preceded by those before us like our parents and followed by those after us, our children.[3]

---

1   Victor E. Frankl, *Man's Search for Meaning* (Boston: Beacon Press, 2006).

2   "Understanding Adoption: A Developmental Approach," *Pediatric Child Health* 6, no. 5 (2001).

3   Lee Roy Beach, *The Psychology of Narrative Thought: How the Stories We Tell Ourselves Shape Our Lives* (Bloomington, IN: Xlibiris, 2010).

But what if we don't know who came before us? And how much of who we are aligns with our genetic features versus the environments we are raised in? And, my personal favorite, how are we supposed to figure out where we belong if we lack narrative structure in our lives?

A great deal of my angst came from the lack of family memory. Having never met my birthmother, I never got to hear the stories of her life. Moreover, my parents never shared an abundance of their own stories either.

In studying how memory passed down from Holocaust survivors, Marianne Hirsch coined the term "post-memory" which she defined as "the memory of the child of the survivor whose life is dominated by memories of what preceded his/her birth."4 Post-memories are what our parents hand down to us. What interests me, though, is the notion that perhaps the lack of these memories influence identity formation, too. By understanding the importance of post-memory in identity development, we can better understand the kind of trauma that occurs when post-memory is absent or with the sudden appearance of a startling new post-memory.

The sudden discovery of post-memory is, in my opinion, best portrayed in a fictional book I read in a literature class focused on genocide and trauma, *The German Mujahid* by Boualem Sansal.5 In it, two protagonists—Rachel and Malrich—stumble upon knowledge of their late father's past as a German SS officer. This discovery is debilitating to each of the brothers' identities, and they contend with it through one

---

4   Marianne Hirsch, "Family Pictures: Maus, Mourning, and Post Memory," *Discourse: Berkeley Journal for Theoretical Studies in Media Culture* 15, no. 2 (1992-93).

5   Boualem Sansal, *The German Mujahid*, trans. Frank Wynne (New York: Europa Editions, 2009).

of the most powerful forms of self-discovery: diaries. Though the brothers come across their father's truth separately and at different times, their traumas illuminate how fragile family narratives can sometimes be when faced with the unexpected.

Scientists have also discovered that we can actually inherit anxiety and depression—even without a marked family history—if our parents have experienced trauma. If enough stress is experienced, the gene encoding for the FK506 binding protein 5 (FKBP5) can change and be passed down. These genetic changes were documented in a study on children of Holocaust survivors.6 But this kind of research is still in its infancy, and there hasn't yet been a study on this kind of genetic inheritance with a control for children who aren't given the gift of traumatic post-memory.

For adopted children like me, there are gaps in our actual memories *and* our post-memories. This makes it difficult to piece together the stories of our lives into a narrative structure that might illuminate some deeper meaning. It isn't often clear the direction we should turn in order to sort these things out.

Everyone thinks that where there are gaps, we should seek out the answers, and in turn, those answers will give us meaning. When I was younger, I wanted to be able to look at my biological past and find something that would make me feel like I had a destiny or a path. But I kept coming up with more questions, more disappointment, and more confusion. My parents tried to convince me that I had been adopted because God wanted something better for me; they seemed to think the deeper meaning should be that I aspire to be the opposite of my genetic history. But I'm a lot like Harry

---

6   Rachel Yehuda et al., "Holocaust Exposure Induced Intergenerational Effects on FKBP5 Methylation," *Biological Psychiatry* 80, no. 5 (2016).

Potter. They couldn't stomp the magic out of me, the bits of unique selfhood born of genetic tendency, the ever-present ache for something more. As I tried to define myself based on spotty information and broken dreams from all three of my parents, I had to face the music. These outside forces couldn't give me true meaning. I am what I am, and I am what I want to be. That's it.

I now believe that instead of seeking out answers, we are in charge of ascribing our own meaning to life. In other words, the meaning that we build our lives upon isn't out there somewhere waiting to be found. It's inside of each and every one of us. All we have to do is recognize our power and take it for ourselves.

In writing this book, I hope to share the experience of desperately seeking answers and coming up blank, what it feels like to fill in a story with gaps, and what it feels like to look for meaning in all the wrong places.

Like the brothers in *The German Mujahid* finding out about a past tainted with shame, the way I looked at my life and the world around me shifted dramatically when I began to grapple with my own biological history. According to Erik Erikson, adolescence (in all its joys) is a critical stage for the development of identity, and mine crumbled in a single afternoon as I looked up words like "schizophrenia," "cocaine," and "bastard" in the dictionary.[7]

The two biggest questions that moved me to compose a fictionalized echo of what my journey could have been were: Who am I? And why am I like this? I hoped to answer those questions as I began to sketch out this book. As I worked

---

7   Erik Erikson, "The Life Cycle: Epigenesis of Identity." In *Identity: Youth and Crisis* (New York: W. W. Norton, 1994).

through my own experience, I ended up with a story about a girl brave enough to ask the questions I'd avoided about my adoption and identity for years.

I want to share this piece of self-discovery with anybody who has dealt with emotional trauma. Whether it's by relating directly to the main character, Izzie, or trying to understand someone else going through something similar, my hope is that this story can help illuminate that there is power to be gained if you're brave enough.

For people who look at their lives honestly and see gaping holes in the narrative, for people who haven't yet found the courage to share their stories, or for anyone else looking for answers in all the wrong places—I hope that this book helps you understand life's big questions and how to make sense of them.

Experience through Izzie's eyes what it feels like to learn new things about oneself and yearn to know more. If you like unicorns, mermaids, the nostalgic tone of the late 2000s, or winding summer road trips, this book is for you. Enjoy.

ROSE'S LOCKET

PART 1

MY ADOPTION

CHAPTER 1

THE BIRTHDAY BLOWOUT

———

It was my eighteenth birthday, and like all the rest of my birthdays, the usual plans were in the works. That morning my mom had set out the camera on the kitchen table, the cake box mix on the counter, and a pile of small gifts on the fireplace. I didn't yet know what was going to go wrong, but I could feel in my bones that it would be something colossal.

As far back as I could remember, my mom approached life idealistically. She looked at our lives as a series of carefully posed pictures in scrapbooks—moments planned for and curated and sealed up in a vacuum of perfection. But our life wasn't like that. Things went wrong, and they always seemed to go wrong in exactly the moments she wanted to be pure. It took me a while to understand this side of her, but if you knew her the way my sister and I do, you'd see the moments missing from the photos or details left out of the memories she's shared. But once you've seen that other side, it's glaring. And it has overshadowed all my memories.

There were times when it wasn't her fault at all, just some kind of cosmic fluke where something didn't go the way it should have. There's not a single event I can recall that went according to plan. Once, when I won a writing contest in elementary school, I sneezed in the middle of the picture she took, and it was the last photo on the roll of film. And, of course, there was the time that she planned a huge scavenger hunt for me, my sister, and all my friends for my birthday—but it rained. We had to help clean up all the soggy treats from the backyard the next day.

I could go on and on about the strange string of bad luck that seemed to follow me on my birthdays, but I could never put my finger on why they felt like such strained celebrations. There was something off about them, but I never quite knew what. And I definitely didn't know how to explain that feeling of quiet dread inside me that arose once a year.

It wasn't just good plans gone wrong; there were entire gaps of memory that I knew were being held beyond my reach. Gaps of memory that, like the discarded pictures of life that weren't pretty enough for her scrapbook, had been erased. But it wasn't only the suppression of the story that bothered me. It was who had owned the narrator's voice for so long.

On my sixteenth birthday, two years ago, my bad birthday luck hit again. I was sent home from school with a stomach virus. When I got home, a letter for me was in the mailbox, and a package with my name sat by the front door. I brought them inside, set them on the kitchen counter, saw my mom asleep on the couch, and went to my room to take a nap. I didn't look at the mail closely; I assumed they were gifts from aunts or uncles, and I felt too sick to care. Later on, when I woke up, both the letter and the package had disappeared. When I asked about them, my mom told me not to worry.

"We'll talk about this when you're ready, Isabell."

At dinner that night, when I said, "I'm ready to talk about it now," she simply frowned at my dad and shook her head at me. I had a pretty good hunch then that they were from my birthmother. Why else would a letter and package be hidden from me? I wasn't polite or quiet about my irritation with my parents for keeping this from me so blatantly, but they held their ground and reminded me that when I was ready, they would tell me more about my birthmother and the other things they admitted they'd received from her. I'd left the house that night to spend the rest of the evening with my boyfriend, Matt, who did his best to console me despite not quite understanding the complexities of my adoption angst.

I was adopted as a baby, but the story as it was always told to me was patchy, like the missing photographs in a scrapbook, and I knew I hadn't been told everything. My parents had read a few letters aloud to me, but I'd never held anything in my hands. The story of my adoption—the way they told it—always sounded like a fairytale. It was something unexplainable and magical, something that could only have been orchestrated by God himself.

Once upon a time, my parents would tell me, a woman in San Antonio got pregnant. She was not married; she had clearly made a mistake. Something else was wrong, but I'd never been told what. And anyway, those details weren't so important. It was what she did *after* realizing she was pregnant that was important.

This woman prayed and prayed that God would lead her toward the right decision for the baby. Her father pushed for adoption, and so the woman checked herself into a facility where she could live during the pregnancy and choose adoptive parents from a large filing cabinet of applicants.

Around the same time, at a church convention somewhere in the West Texas panhandle in the early fall of 1989, a preacher's wife looked across the room to the woman who would soon be my mom and knew that she had something important to tell her.

"God told me you're going to have a baby," the preacher's wife said, and my mom, a quiet teacher who longed for the laughter of little children, didn't know what to say. She couldn't get the moment out of her head.

When she came home, my dad hugged her and said, "I hope she's right."

During a church event a few weeks later, my dad prayed that—like the preacher's wife had said—they would soon be parents. Like a bolt of lightning, a line of thought came to him. When he went home, he put that line in a letter and sent it off to the adoption agency along with all the other required materials.

In a strangely inspired moment sometime after this in November, the pregnant woman at the adoption center saw the file of the parents she would choose. This was a very big moment for everybody in the story. When she met the couple—pictured with their little white dog—she would tell them it was the following line in their letter that drew her to them for the little lifeform growing inside her: "We want to wrap your child in the love of Jesus Christ."

But for the woman who was pregnant with this little child, the story falls off a bit. My parents never told me what happened between November and April. All I know is that I was born somewhere in San Antonio, then came home with my parents soon after to try to fulfill some kind of idyllic life path. The story always ended with some sentiment about how I was meant for great things, things I wouldn't have had the opportunity to achieve unless God had put me where I belonged.

And maybe that was true, but I didn't like that the story ended with such finality. What about the rest of my life? Where was I supposed to be going? And what was my birthmother like? Would I be like her? Questions like this plagued me, but my parents were especially tight-lipped about it. "You're right where God wants you to be," they'd tell me. But soon, I wouldn't need anybody's permission to dig up the past and find out what they hadn't been telling me. First, though, I had to get through my eighteenth birthday.

* * *

The house was quiet when I got home but smelled like the warm remnants of baking. My birthday cake, freshly frosted, was ready on the counter. We all sat down at the table to eat, and nothing went wrong. It was uncanny. The brisket didn't burn, the frosting on the cake was perfect, and the conversation centered around how my friends had helped me celebrate at school. As the extrovert of the family, I could tell an engaging dinner story or two. That night I knew I had a little leeway to let slip a sliver of shenanigans without getting in trouble since it was my birthday. But I found it particularly difficult to stay present and enjoy the nice time we had at the dinner table as I talked and my family laughed; picture-perfect moments have always felt surreal to me, and this one was no different. I was terrified that if I enjoyed the moment just a little too much, sadness would envelop me afterward. That's how it always happened for me, anyway.

After dinner, we sat down in the living room to open all my presents. Nothing crazy. This was the routine in my family. Our home life was a quiet affair. My parents never had many friends they were comfortable inviting to the house, and it wasn't very often my sister and I were allowed to host sleepovers. When my boyfriend, Matt, would come over, we had to stay in the living room for family time, which was usually awkward for everybody. While there wasn't anything wrong with quiet lives or birthdays, I always felt like something was missing. That would change when I got out and on my own. I was so close, I could almost taste the freedom.

After opening my gifts, my parents looked at each other and nodded.

"Isabell," my dad said, "we have one last thing for you now that you're eighteen." I glanced at my blonde younger sister— Veronica, or as we called her, Ronnie—who was adopted, too. Though opposites, we shared psychic moments sometimes. Our sisterhood was a delicate thing. But with one look, I knew we had the same reaction to our dad's announcement. This was the voice of gravity. The voice of a man handing over car keys for the first time or explaining the importance of curfew. She raised one eyebrow at me, and her green eyes gleamed with curiosity.

Looking back at my dad, I leaned forward. What could it possibly be? He gave a smile to my mom, who pulled out a large folder filled with papers. She handed it over to me, carefully keeping eye contact with me as if to signal that there should be no outbursts, no emotional questions.

"It's time for you to have some of the letters from your birthmother," she said. "You know we have always told you that God blessed us with you. But... we understand if you are curious to know more."

I reached out immediately to take it. She held on for a brief moment before relinquishing it to me. Before opening the folder, I looked at both of my parents. Their faces were painted with the red-handedness of being caught in a moment they didn't have the words to better navigate—a moment they always knew would come but didn't want to face until forced. I glanced again at my sister, and she moved closer to glimpse the contents. In three years, my parents would probably hand her the same kind of folder with all the details of her own adoption.

When I finally opened it, letters and pictures fell out. I set them aside. A part of me knew letters had been hidden from me. But what was the rest of this?

The first page was a biographical sheet with my birth-mother's name at the top: *Carole Anne*. I scanned through race, height, eye color, and religious affiliation to the bottom. Addictions. "Cocaine, PCP, acid, marijuana," I read aloud. "What's PCP?"

My mom pursed her lips, sweeping her auburn hair out of her face. "God sent you to us for a reason," she said quietly.

I looked at her blankly. "Are you going to answer the question?"

"It's a drug," she responded bluntly.

"What does it do?"

"I don't know, Isabell." She frowned at me, then got up and motioned to my dad, who followed her back to the kitchen. I flipped through the pages to gauge what I'd been given. Biographical sheets in a small loopy handwriting, actual adoption paperwork including my parents' letter asking for a child, two questionnaires filled out by them, and a printed map to the adoption agency. When I finally looked up, my mom held out something else. It was a small navy-blue box.

I reached out for it but paused. "Was this what was in that package when I turned sixteen?" I asked sharply. It was no secret that I had been livid at my mom that day.

She nodded. "Yes, you are ready now."

I scoffed, taking the box from her. Inside was a golden locket shaped like a heart with a tiny red rose on the front and a little folded note tucked behind it. The note read: *My grandmother gave this to me, and I want you to have it.* The locket was empty inside but also a little scuffed on the back. I turned it over in my hands, then handed it to my sister, who fastened it around my neck. I began to gather up all the papers and pictures to put back in the folder. After all, I preferred to brood over these documents in the safety of my room.

My mom reached out for the folder expectantly.

I raised my eyebrows, pulling the folder close against my chest.

Her lips thinned determinedly as she held her hands out. "Isabell, you can look through those now, but you have to give them back. They're not yours."

"They're not mine? The pictures of me and details about my birthmother aren't mine?" I challenged.

Her brow furrowed. Her lip quivered. Was she going to yell or cry? I could never tell which was oncoming, but I could tell she was getting upset. I wasn't reacting the right way to a moment she'd spent eighteen years planning.

"We want to keep these things safe for you. I've seen your room; you can't keep anything nice. Half your books have cheese fingerprints in them. Now give it back if you're done looking."

I laughed scathingly. "Oh, no. You're not getting this back. You've kept this stuff from me for eighteen years. There's no way in hell I'm giving it back to you. God only knows what kind of dirt is in here that you've been too afraid to tell me."

"Isabell," my dad interjected, his tone warning. His brown eyes, usually so warm, flashed at me dangerously. They had lightened along with his hair over the years, and now they burned orange with annoyance.

"Don't 'Isabell' me. You don't think this is shitty? There's more to what happened than God sending me to you in a woven basket. And if you think I'm going to hand this over, you're very, *very* wrong."

My mom burst into tears, starting toward me as if to forcibly remove the folder. I stood up, folder clasped in both hands.

"Isabell. I'm serious. Either sit back down and look through it or hand it over," my mom said as she inched toward me. Her face was red; tears were beginning to bubble over in glassy puddles at the bottoms of her eyelids. I'd never seen this version of determined and upset from her before, and it bewildered me.

"No." I bolted. My mom sprinted after me. I blasted through the front door like a tipped firework and ran out to my car but realized too late that I'd forgotten my keys inside. My mom took this opportunity to pounce, grab me by the elbow, and try to rip the folder out of my hands. Ronnie screamed at her to let me go. I violently elbowed until she let go of me, then I looked down the street.

"Don't you dare," she breathed. But it was too late. I had already set off sprinting down the street in my bare feet, determined to get as far away as possible.

I ran out of the neighborhood into the field separating our housing division from the school district. I sprinted all the way down the street to my old junior high. Once there, I crawled up onto the roof of the southern building and hid behind the row of air conditioning units before catching my breath.

My feet ached from the roughness of dirt paths and worn-out asphalt. My bare soles were practically black. And my chest was heaving. But I felt alive and free in that moment.

They would never find me. A good rule of thumb for living in a small town where gossip is actually printed in the newspaper: always have two hiding spots, one you can get to by foot and one you can get to by car.

Unfortunately, I would have to return at some point to the ambush probably waiting for me at home. I didn't have my keys or my phone—just the clothes on my back and a folder full of information. But the sun hadn't set yet, so I decided to rifle through the artifacts in peace before trudging back to another fight. There was no way in hell I would let anybody touch this paperwork.

I was right about one thing, though. Something catastrophic had happened today, and this time it wasn't just bad birthday luck. How could I ever forgive my parents for keeping these things from me? The more I paged through documents that told a thousand stories I'd never been told before, the more I could feel the rift between my parents and me crack farther open.

CHAPTER 2

DOCUMENTS AND DETAILS

I pored over the folder's information as deliberately as possible. For as curious as I was about all the details, finding them proved hard. Diamonds were buried deep in the thick mud of paperwork. I tried to skim—as best as I could—through the legal jargon, the social worker's notes from home visits, and informational pamphlets about the adoption agency. I thanked my lucky stars the evening wasn't windy as I laid out in piles the different kinds of papers. Letters in one pile, pictures in another, legal documents here, filled-out forms there.

Finally, one of the letters caught my attention.

March 29, 2006
Dear Quince Family,

Happy birthday, Rose Isabell! I hope you like the gift that accompanies this letter. I'm sorry it's been a long time since I've written. I'm living with my boyfriend now and saving up to buy a car. I live on Social Security because I've had a mental disability since 1992 (paranoid schizophrenia). I take medication—a shot that lasts a month, kind of like the twenty-four-hour medications we take. Only this lasts in the blood a whole month, distributing little by little. It helps, and socially I'm quite a bit better. I've searched for Rose Isabell's father in the phone book but haven't gotten through yet. I have a few more to call. His name is Jesus. I wonder when I get in touch with him if he can write. I have no pictures of myself at this time, but I'd love to see some pictures of Rose Isabell.

Love,
Carole

I didn't know what to do with this information. What was paranoid schizophrenia? In what way did that diagnosis make her disabled? I would have to look this up in the dictionary when I got home. And who was Rose Isabell? Me? I looked again at the golden heart-shaped locket around my neck, the gift. Alongside the little red rose engraved on the front were the words *I love you.*

Finally, as the sun began to set, I carefully rearranged everything and put it neatly back together. I didn't know how to feel about any of it. Was the little baby in those pictures the same human I looked at every day in the mirror? Who was this woman who had birthed me, and why didn't I know anything about her? I didn't think I looked at all like the woman in those pictures.

As I trudged my way back through town and across the dirt path in the field to my neighborhood, I contemplated burying my treasure somewhere but ultimately decided against it. I only had my hands, and the earth was dry and brittle. My heart felt like it could crack open, too, like the barren pieces of sod falling apart beneath my dirty feet.

I would have to argue when I got home. Maybe I would have to fight. They would be waiting up for me like they always did when I took off like this. I was what you could call a "flight risk."

The first time I ran, it was because I wanted to go to a junior high dance. I wanted to wear short shorts and a tight t-shirt and dance with all my friends. It had been too much for my mom to handle. After all the conversations we'd had about how virginity is a gift from God that I should save for my husband, I still wanted to kiss boys. So, the night of the dance, she grounded me for getting a B in math. I saw through this ploy immediately, went to bed early, and crawled out the window. When I walked home after an exhilarating night of dancing—the first time I'd ever felt really alive—my dad was silently waiting on the curb. He didn't say a word as we walked the rest of the way home together, but I got an earful from my mom the next day.

My parents and I always struggled to see eye-to-eye. I had an adventurer's soul from the moment I could walk, but my parents seemed content to live a quiet life at home with clearly defined rules. Growing up, I didn't understand why. Why did we learn in Sunday school that God loved us as we were, but then had to turn around and wear pantyhose every Sunday? Why were so many things off-limits? When would I have the freedom to explore the world? Why didn't my mom understand that I didn't want to be the same kind of woman she was? I didn't want to wear dresses or cross my legs demurely. I wanted to be out in the wild world in overalls and a ponytail seeing all there was to see.

But despite all the times my parents and I had argued over things like this, I wasn't deterred. If anything, I was more determined to bust out of the box they'd built for me. Something was missing in my life, something I could only find in the dead of night. It was the feeling of actually having control over my world, the feeling of unadulterated freedom. My whole life, I'd been boxed in. Boxed in at home and at church—the only two places the rest of my family wanted to be. But I wanted something more.

When I fell in love with my boyfriend, Matt, in ninth grade, he gave me some of that freedom. We would stroll along the sidewalks at three in the morning, climb over neighbors' fences to swim in their pools, and take liquor that wouldn't be missed from his parents' cabinet. Even his family felt more open. They let me curse and watch R-rated movies. They let me buy racy t-shirts when we went shopping. And though Matt didn't usually offer up much in the way of contemplation on complex matters like my adoption, he was good at listening.

Walking along the road, I thought about how much I missed him. He was a year older than me, so for my whole senior year, he was away at college. We were bound to phone calls, emails, and letters. Texting was too expensive. But sometimes our conversations went dark for a week or two at a time. That's when I worried the most. Maybe the long-distance thing wouldn't work. But he always came back to me. Two weeks was the longest we'd ever gone without talking. And once I graduated, I could follow him to school. Studying what, I didn't know, but at least I would be near him again, and more importantly, I would be free.

I really hoped, as I approached home, that nobody would be waiting for me so that I could get my pack of cigarettes from the knot in the tree on the side of our house and sneak a smoke in the park. But I had a feeling this time wouldn't be like the rest. The sinking feeling in my belly turned out to be right as I turned the corner to my street. My parents were sitting in fold-out chairs on the lawn waiting for me.

I clutched the folder close to my chest, deliberately slowing down. I needed to know more, and I knew their lips would be sealed tight—but I had to ask my questions anyway.

While details had been somewhat illuminated in the contents of this folder, there were gaps. Would my parents answer my questions? I drew deep breaths as I gathered my courage.

As I got closer to the house, my mom stood up and began walking toward me. I tensed, ready to run again, though I didn't know where I'd go. All I knew was that I wouldn't let her take this paperwork from me. She walked toward me until we met on the sidewalk in front of our neighbor's house.

"Izzie," she said to me gently. "I know you're upset. But you have to understand."

I didn't say anything, waiting for her to finish her thought. It didn't come. She looked at me expectantly, but I kept walking toward the house. She followed me.

"You know we love you, that God loves you," she began again. "And we just wanted you to be old enough to handle all of this. That's why we kept it from you."

We'd arrived at the front door, my dad trailing behind us.

"We're sure you have lots of questions," he offered as he held open the door.

Hesitantly, I stepped through and turned to walk back to my bedroom. Maybe, after having the evening to think about it, they'd reconsidered. They both seemed calmer, after all.

"Wait," my mom said as she put her hand on my shoulder. "Aren't you forgetting?"

I cocked my head at her.

"You need to give us back those documents."

My breath shaking, I smiled. "No, Mom. These are mine now. But if you'd like to go through them one more time and answer my questions, we can do that at the kitchen table."

My mom's eyes began to fill with tears again; my dad stepped in to reply.

"That would be great."

We went to sit at the kitchen table, facing each other. I put the folder down without taking my hand from atop it as I sat down. This was my moment, and I wasn't ready for it at all.

My mom reached across the table for the folder, but I slid it back toward me and held it against my chest.

"I just thought you said we could…?" she asked.

"I meant that *I* would hold the paperwork and ask *you* questions about it," I said sternly.

Her lips tightened, and my dad sighed. They both took deep breaths, readying themselves for what they knew I might ask.

I opened the folder to the pile of letters. There weren't that many. My birthmother, Carole, had only written sporadically. I didn't need to look at the fragile pieces of notebook paper to ask my questions, though. The letters gave me the context to better understand some of the dry facts.

"The biographical sheets," I began. "If you had these from the beginning, why didn't you tell me about them in fourth grade when I had that heritage assignment?"

"Don't you remember?" my mom asked.

"I remember crying and bringing an English dish to class."

"We told you that we might have that information. The only thing is, we don't know how much of this information is accurate. It's limited," she said.

"You don't believe what's written here?"

"The way adoption works, we don't get actual medical records, so we only have what she wrote down on those forms to go off," my mom explained. "And it was the same when we found out about the mental disorder; it was just in a letter she wrote."

"The mental disorder?"

"Well, yes. Paranoid schizophrenia. It's…"

"What are the symptoms?"

My dad spoke up. "It varies. We don't really know what her exact symptoms were, only that she was diagnosed with paranoid schizophrenia in 1992. We actually didn't know about that diagnosis until she wrote us that letter talking about it later on. The most common symptom is… hallucinations."

"Hallucinations? What do you mean? Is it genetic? Could I get it, too?"

They looked at each other. An unspoken conversation spanning lifetimes happened immediately in front of me.

"It—" my mom started nervously.

"It can be inherited," my dad interjected. "It usually passes down through the mother's side. But not always. The symptoms don't usually appear until early adulthood, around twenty years old."

I temporarily forgot what else I was going to ask. A heavy silence fell over us all. I felt gutted, wondering if I would inherit schizophrenia, too. Hallucinations?

I tried to regroup. "Why don't you just start from the beginning and tell me the whole story." I started flipping through the folder nervously. "Like, tell me what you know about her. I've heard the 'God sent me' story a thousand times."

"But it's true, and now that you know that she struggled with… schizophrenia and… and drugs, well," my mom said. "God sent you to us for a reason."

I did my best not to roll my eyes.

"Carole did a good and noble thing. God gave you to us so you could be different," she said.

"But tell me about the drugs. I just have a list here: cocaine, marijuana, PCP, acid. I don't know what half of those things are. What do they do?"

"Isabell. All you need to know is that those things are bad, and that isn't your path. You can have a different life," she said sternly, then looked to my dad. He nodded.

"Just tell me what you know."

"We don't know much," my dad said.

"Well, tell me what you *do* know."

To my surprise, they moved past their usual story and began to recount what they remembered. They told me that during Carole's stay at the adoption agency home, she ate canned spinach because she thought that, like Popeye, it might help the baby in her belly grow strong. They told me that when I was born, Carole called me Rose, which was why she addressed me that way in her letters. Despite this, they brought me home and named me Isabell which means "God as my oath." The reason they chose that name, they said, was because I was God's fulfilled promise to them that they would be parents. But as they explained this, I couldn't help but get stuck on the name Rose.

"I didn't know I was called Rose. Why didn't you tell me that?"

"It was what she called you, but we wanted to name you Isabell," my mom said.

I didn't know how to feel about this and sat quietly, eyebrows furrowed in thought as my parents continued with their story.

They explained that the years in between letters usually meant that Carole had fallen off the deep end in drugs or didn't have a permanent address, which was obvious by the content of her letters. Though they sent Christmas letters every year to the adoption agency to send on to her, many were returned to them.

And when I asked about my biological father, a man Carole hadn't left many details about on his bio sheet, they shrugged their shoulders and said darkly that they hadn't been married. There were many decisions she had made that they didn't approve of.

When they fell back into telling me the same old story of God putting me in their lives, I placed everything back in the folder and stood. I wanted the mystical God story to stop interrupting the truth. I was happy for the new pieces of information but still didn't understand why God was always the end-all answer to the background of my adoption. I was only eighteen years old; it didn't make sense that they'd already wrapped up my story with a bow and called it complete.

"You are meant to be better than she was," my mom said with a tone of satisfied finality. But this comment snapped something deep inside of me.

"Who am I supposed to be like? *You*?"

My mom gasped, completely bewildered. My dad frowned.

"You've kept all of this from me. For eighteen years, you've told me the same story over and over again. I'm *special*, I'm *chosen*, I'm God's fulfilled promise to you. But it sounds like I'm the product of a drugged-up one-night stand, and you were too ashamed to tell me it happened that way. What, were you scared I'd turn out like her? Scared that if I found out about the drugs that I would go try them out?"

"N-no, Isabell. We want better for you. We—"

"Then why did you keep all this from me? You don't want better for me. You want to control me. You always have. And you can't."

My mom sobbed as my dad gave me a stony, stoic look. I could feel my cheeks beginning to burn, half from frustration and half from the terrifying thrill of having spoken to my parents this way.

"We thought it would be better this way," he said. "But maybe we were wrong."

"Maybe so," I snapped. I scooped up the folder and left them in the kitchen. Though they'd been more open with me than they had ever been in my entire life, their explanations still felt stifled. I felt displaced knowing that I could never, would never be what they wanted me to be.

When I got to my room, there was a missed call from Matt on my cell phone. I called him back, hoping for a friendly voice to remind me that things were okay, but he didn't pick up. I didn't want to leave a voicemail for fear my voice would crack as I tried to explain. Feeling more alone than I ever had before, I hung up and lay in my bed staring at the ceiling fan as it slowly turned. I contemplated sending a text message but, knowing that it cost extra and that my parents would be furious, I decided against it. I didn't have the energy to put up a fight for a stupid text message.

I slept with the folder under my pillow and, all night, dreamed of a woman like me. One who wrote poetry when she was drunk, who wanted a bigger life experience, whose baby was taken away from her after she was convinced that she wasn't good enough to be a mother, a woman whose head I desperately wanted to get inside.

* * *

As a little kid, I always wondered why adults were so obsessed with talking about the weather. At the grocery store, after church, even on vacation—the topic was always the weather. I didn't get it.

But after sitting in my thoughts the month that followed my April birthday, I did.

You never know what to expect, what kind of sky you'll wake up to, what kind of disaster or delight will guide you through the day. And all of April had been a flickering of rain and sunshine and wind and chill, all one after the other, for me. Blink, blink, blink. A different day, a different mood. And all of them were meaningless in the chaos of broken story pieces that surrounded me.

A couple of days after my birthday, I wrote Matt a short letter to let him know what had happened. I didn't take the time to plan out what I wanted to write the way I usually did; instead, I scrawled some half-assed explanation and sent it off. I didn't think he'd understand the situation, so I didn't see any reason to elaborate.

Right before I wrote the letter, he called my cell phone while I was in school. He left a cheery voicemail, but every time I called him back, he didn't answer. Somehow, almost an entire month passed this way, back and forth between voicemails of no substance. If I didn't know better, I might have thought he was only calling when he knew I was busy. I had never felt more frustrated with the distance between us.

Beyond that, I'd taken to putting together the pieces of my life the only way I knew how. I bought a bright pink one-inch binder, some card stock, stick glue, and sheet protectors. Whether I liked to admit it or not, I was a lot like my mom. Here I was with no clue what to do, absolutely overloaded with too much information, and I was scrapbooking. What was wrong with me?

I couldn't help but look at Carole's handwriting, the different scrawls from different years. One of the earliest was printed neatly, characters carefully looped. I could tell by the neatness that she put a lot of thought into how to tell me of her years of drinking and drug use, and the pain of poverty. By that point, I'd read the lines over and over.

October 9, 1997
Dear Mr. & Mrs. Quince,

So long since I've written. I got caught up in drinking and drugging for about four years and recently gave it up to serve the Lord again. I'm living with some friends and saving up for a car right now. I want to hear from you. Please send pictures of Rose Isabell and send her all my love.

Love,
Carole

The letters of later years devolved into a scrawl, something hastily written at the Post Office where she bought both the card and stamp.

May 12, 2002
Dear Isabell Rose,

Sorry if this reaches you late. I hope you had a happy, joyous birthday with some happy surprises. I pray you are growing in stature and grace with the Lord. Love yourself and others second.

I love you,
Carole

But those letters were outliers from the rest of the documents in the folder. Most of what I'd seen inside told a completely different story. I also had letters that my parents wrote to their friends, pictures of me as a baby with the lawyer who helped with paperwork, and pictures of a social worker holding me.

But even with all this information, there was no guiding light to tie it all together. My parents never offered up a cohesive narrative. And Carole had only given some of her story through those short letters. Somewhere outside of that pile of papers was my story, yet it wasn't even mine.

Probably the most revealing part of all the documentation was the pile of bio sheets on all of my extended relatives. Carole was asked to fill out these sheets to provide a greater biological and social context. On the front of each page were biological statistics. What race? How tall? Eye color? It reminded me of science class in fourth grade when we learned about genetics, as if learning that I would bleed for half my life wasn't trauma enough. Our teacher told us all to ask our parents about our heritage and bring a food dish from that culture. I went home crying. I didn't know my bloodline and ended up bringing something from my dad's heritage, some kind of English pastry. For a moment, even if it was short-lived, I felt more whole listening to my dad nostalgically describe the family's renaming at Ellis Island for no reason other than there were too many Johnsons already. And I understood how he felt. It's important to be proud of where you came from. But most of the time, it felt like I came from nowhere.

But I guessed that, according to this paperwork, I came from some mixture of places: Germany, France, and England plus a mysterious "Mexico?" scrawled on my birthfather's bio sheet. My birthmother didn't seem to know much about him. Just as well.

Once I'd organized the papers and photographs in some semblance of order, it seemed to me that—after spending a lifetime wondering what was missing from my story—suddenly knowing more felt strangely empty.

I couldn't help but wonder about my future now that I had more of my past than I'd ever had before. I didn't know why, but the past and the future seemed so ominously connected. I couldn't shake the numbing fear that there might be parts of me, maybe hereditary parts of me, that simply couldn't be fought.

I thought about the way my parents shared that glance of a lifetime at the kitchen table when I'd asked about paranoid schizophrenia. I wondered if they feared that I too would exhibit symptoms and fall off the edge of the earth, unable to function, unable to make them proud. Maybe they meant to shield me from that fear, but it had come for me anyway.

Although I knew it was too much to process all at once, I couldn't help but feel that all the new information I'd amassed still wasn't enough. Time seemed to have stopped for me, to live this moment endlessly. The sky kept changing, but I hadn't woken up yet. I didn't feel like anybody—not Isabell or Rose or Izzie or anyone. I was just existing in some small-framed body of a brown-haired girl with freckles and blue eyes, who had been dropped out of nowhere into this lifetime.

I didn't understand how my parents existed so quietly, without a sound. I might be loud as hell, but I told the truth, even when nobody wanted to hear it. I didn't get how they could lie. How could they keep all of this from me? I'd been looking at every detail of all of these documents obsessively; wasn't the information about me supposed to be a part of me? Part of my story? Part of the reason I was who I was? Who I would become?

But I'd had it with scrapbooking. I needed to check on the weather. I was going to run away. For real this time.

CHAPTER 3

THE ESCAPE TO
THE LAKE

———

It wasn't that hard to run away. I knew where my parents would never find me. After all that had happened when I turned eighteen, the house began to shrink. I desperately needed an escape beyond school. I could feel the walls moving in on me. The tension in the air was so thick, I often thought about how easy it would be to spread it on toast, serve it up for breakfast, and poison us all. Both my parents and Ronnie walked on eggshells around me; I felt like they were all just waiting for me to snap, but I didn't give them the satisfaction. Instead, I fell further into my head and wondered where on earth I could go to find some peace and quiet to think about all the information that had been dropped in my lap.

Every time I mustered up the courage to ask my parents a new question, I got vague answers. Or worse, lectures. The buzzing of anxiety that filled our house quickly grew unbearable. I needed to get away.

On a Saturday morning in May, a full month after my birthday, I packed up water bottles, snacks, camping gear, and some clothes into my car. My dad was at work, my mom was volunteering at the church, and Ronnie was still asleep. I didn't leave a note when I left; there wasn't anything I could say that I thought my parents would understand.

The morning was still new, the dew shining on the grass blades in the reflection of a bright sunrise. Though it wasn't yet hot, a cloudless sky promised it would be soon. On my way out of the driveway, I checked the mail just in case Matt had written back. We'd exclusively communicated through short voicemails for too long. I couldn't tell if something was wrong or if I was just upset about not hearing from him because I needed to talk to him so desperately. Two weeks was the longest we'd gone between talking before, but somehow a month had passed. I'd written him a letter, then a couple of emails, but all remained unanswered.

It turned out that Matt had, in fact, responded to me, probably after getting frustrated at not being able to reach me by phone. A white envelope sat in the mailbox with my name on it. It's fun to get letters in the mail, but there's also a kind of emptiness in them. Unspoken things that, no matter how much you attempt to pin them down, just never come out right. Good letters are hard to write, and in this case, I wasn't particularly thrilled to have a piece of paper when I really wanted a phone call. I scooped the letter out of the mailbox, leaving the rest, and drove out of town toward the lake.

Driving, once I'd been set free with a license, turned into a soothing experience. I always tried my best to soak it in. On one of our winding drives to pass the time, Ronnie speculated that driving helped me feel as though I was moving at the same pace as my thoughts. I liked that idea. It *did* feel easier for me to navigate my thoughts as I zoomed down an empty highway with the stereo blaring. I didn't know why. Maybe she was right.

As I drove, I tried to call Matt again, but the phone rang and rang until I got his voicemail. I hung up and decided to listen to Hoobastank's first album, a burned CD that Matt had decorated with a Sharpie for me when we had first met. Though he wasn't especially talented at demonstrating his love for me through words, he did excel in gift-giving. I didn't require much. Burned CDs and stolen trinkets topped the list of my favorite items from him.

I was in a weird mood, and the weather seemed to be mocking me. The sun rapidly rose over the empty plains outside of town, but I couldn't appreciate the brightness of the sunny day. Instead, I felt like my brain was sitting in the eye of a thunderous and violent storm. Though I felt upset with my parents for how they'd handled my adoption information, I also felt strangely calm knowing that they wouldn't be able to find me until I was ready to be found. Despite my marked history of running away and sneaking out, I'd never planned something like this that wasn't just for the fun of it. I wasn't sneaking off to a dance or to drink with my friends—I was running away because I no longer felt safe or understood at home. It felt vindicated and justified that I would put my parents through a little bit of worry for what they'd done to me, not just on my birthday but over my lifetime.

As I drove across the gleaming black highway, I thought about the major differences between my parents and myself. Their beliefs dominated their actions. Christianity defined both the way they told my story and withheld information. I grew up in the church and, for a long time, I was satisfied. The moral code was strong, the experiences were sturdy, and the community was a sustaining source of energy. But as I grew, I began asking questions. For a while, that was okay, too. "God can handle your questions," my mom told me. But God isn't the kind of entity to drop a line now and again. I began to think that the only reason God could handle my questions was because, like any invisible force, he wasn't required to answer them.

I wanted to know why I was taught to be ashamed of my body, why curse words were such a bad thing, why I wasn't allowed to indulge in secular media, why I was told not to judge people in a community that always seemed to be judging people, and why answers to big questions always ended with some vague "because of God" explanation. While my dad would sometimes admit that he didn't have the answers to my questions, my mom became increasingly irritated with me. And now, I had to try and untangle their Christian narrative from a pile of facts that told in glimpses a completely new story.

As Hoobastank began their last song on the album, I pulled into the park adjacent to Lake Coyote. Matt loved this lake. Honestly, it wasn't anything special. When it comes to the lake, it's best described as a large pond that lies at the end of a very shabby creek. It's not big by any means, and I've never seen any clear water. There's a funny smell about the whole park, and the grounds are usually littered with trash. And yet, it's one of his favorite places on earth. We took one another's virginity there and spent many nights drunk and laughing with our friends around a campfire.

I slowed the car down to look out across the greenish hue of the surface as it shone under the sun. Instead of picking a campsite, I continued past the civilized recreation areas and up the creek where the path turned wild. Nobody but hooligans ever came out this far. Though the cops were aware that we came out here to misbehave, they had trouble catching us at it because the footpaths were so winding, so we always got away. I hid my car in the underbrush and assembled the few items I would take with me. While I didn't have a tent, I did have a hammock that I figured would be enough for the night. With gear in my backpack, I set out to follow the footpath a mile or two farther down the creek where the trees were thickest.

There wasn't much setting up to do once I'd decided on a spot to hide out in. Overlooking the water, a wall of trees would hide me decently well if anyone else decided to walk this way. I tied up the hammock, hung my backpack full of food and other essentials on a conveniently placed branch just adjacent, and stripped down.

Though it was an early morning at the beginning of May, the heat was already pretty intense. I didn't bring a ton of clothes so it would be easier to hang out nude in the shade during the day, dip into the creek if I got too hot, and put clothes on for the night when it cooled down.

I crawled into the hammock with Matt's letter and settled in to read. As always, I took a moment to appreciate the way he had scrawled my name in tiny letters on the front of the envelope. I don't know why I love it so much, but something about seeing my name written by someone else makes me feel whole.

When I opened the envelope, a sheet of yellow legal paper was inside along with two dollars and a white note-card that read: *Good for one free back massage. Does not expire.* I tucked these under my thigh so that I could read the letter.

Izzie,

Happy Birthday! Sorry this letter is so late, but when I was about to send you your original birthday letter (also late, sorry!), I got your letter in the mail. It sat on my bathroom counter every day for an entire week, and I read it over and over again, trying to think of what to say. I really wish we could catch each other on the phone, but I guess this will have to do. I'm sorry we keep missing each other.

I actually remember when that locket you mentioned came in the mail because you were so pissed that you hadn't opened both the package and the envelope when you had the chance. Is it weird to receive a family heirloom from someone you never knew? I bet that's nuts.

Maybe you need some boring stuff to get your mind off it. Hopefully, you haven't defaulted to listening to Hoobastank, but if you have, I guess I can't really blame you. This is crazy.

So. The boring stuff. I'm almost done with the semester. Just have to finish up my final projects, all of which involve some stupid explanatory essay describing WHY I chose to do the project. Like, I get why the professors want those explanations, but it's also such a pain in the ass to build something and then have to explain it afterward. Once that stuff is done, though, I'll be heading home. Everything is due in two weeks, but if we finish early, we're allowed to leave. So yeah, hopefully, I can be home sooner.

I've also been working on a secret project that I haven't told you about yet. Since you're graduating this year, I wanted to give you something special. I know we've kind of wandered around the subject of what you're planning to do after graduation, and I know that, as of the last time we talked about it, you were thinking of taking a gap year. So, I'm in the process of making you some handmade journals that you can document your adventures in while you're out doing whatever kids do on gap years. Or hell, you could use them for whatever. I know I'm kind of spoiling the surprise by telling you about them, but whatever.

Anyway, I'll be home about a week or so after you get this letter in the mail, and I can't wait to see you. I've really missed you. I really need a night out at the lake. Maybe you do, too. See you soon.

Love,
Matt

P.S. Use the money to go buy some scratch-off tickets. You're legal now!

Tucking the letter, the money, and the notecard back into the envelope, I smiled. Maybe it was that it had been ages since we'd really talked, but that letter resonated with me in a way that most of his other letters didn't. He was never great at putting his emotions into words, but there were times when he surprised me. This was one. We were okay. I had let my worst fears get the best of me. Still, I wanted to get him on the phone soon.

But even without the promise of a phone call or a date to look forward to, I thought about how, once he arrived home, he would probably ask to go to the lake. There was just something magical about it. I think for him, returning to the water was the best way he knew how to return to me. The only problem was, besides reassurance from this letter and a few voicemails, I wasn't entirely confident he would return to me the same this time.

I got down from my perch in the hammock to put the letter away safely in my backpack and retrieved a bottle of water. Glancing up at the sky, I guessed that it was maybe somewhere around nine or ten in the morning.

I got back into the hammock to muse on what Matt had written to me and listen to the whisper of the creek and the sounds of the birds, and before I knew it, I had fallen asleep.

* * *

When I woke up, I was sweltering from the heat of the day. The locket around my neck was stuck on my chest, sticky with sweat. I carefully lifted it, looking closely. I wasn't usually a big fan of jewelry, but this locket was something I didn't think I would ever take off. I felt it was the closest I would ever get to feeling loved just for existing. Maybe that was dumb. I opened and closed it absentmindedly, then decided to sit up and assess the day.

Based on the sun's position, it was early afternoon. Time felt irrelevant though. I hadn't really decided how long I would stay at the lake. I just figured that I would stay as long as I needed to, in order to sort out the thoughts in my head.

Not having a plan somehow made me feel free. Although I liked to plan things the same way my mom did, my streak of spontaneity set me apart, and that made me feel a little more confident about my decision to disappear. I made my way down toward the water. It was too hot to consider being anywhere else. I spent the afternoon alternating between swimming and floating. There were no sounds except for birds in the trees and bugs in the brush.

I wondered what I would tell Matt when he got home. As it stood, I didn't really have a plan of action for anything. I didn't know if I still wanted to take a gap year or if I wanted to start some kind of general studies degree, just to have something to do. Maybe I could just get a job instead and move out. I didn't really want to live in my parents' house anymore. But along with all these meandering semi-plans of what might lie ahead, I also felt like a future would be difficult to define until I really knew more about who I was and what all this information about my birthmother meant.

I wasn't like my parents, that was for sure. But it didn't seem like I was like my birthmother either. Then again, how can you really know what a person is like only through words on paper? Only through informational sheets? It was like peeking in a dusty window at a figure looming just out of sight.

When night finally fell, I put on shorts and a tank top and fell asleep in the hammock, exhausted from both the extensive swimming and all the thinking that still hadn't resulted in a definite plan for anything.

* * *

In the middle of the night, I woke up to people calling my name in the distance. Jolted, I sat up in my hammock and listened as male voices called through the woods to me. It was the cops. As I located the direction of their voices, I could tell that they seemed to be heading my way. Carefully, I slipped out of the hammock and into my tennis shoes. I quietly untied the hammock, stuffed it away, put my backpack on, and headed farther down the creek.

In the time it took me to pack everything up, their voices became louder and I began to see the gleam of their flashlights as they combed through the wilderness. I stepped up my pace to a slow jog, quick enough to get ahead, but slow enough that the sounds of my footsteps might not give me away.

Luckily, I was pretty familiar with this part of the creek, so I knew where the footpath led and when it turned. I also knew that the best way to lose them would be to abandon the footpath at some point and hide, but first I had to get far enough away that they wouldn't hear me breaking branches underfoot.

Back when the cops came out to bust our illicit parties, there was always a designated scapegoat. The only rule of the scapegoat was that you had to be loud and fast so that the cops would chase you while everybody else bolted to more secure hiding places. You needed to be fast because you essentially had to outrun the cops instead of hide. On those nights there were only ever two cops, and they'd never figured out how to effectively team up against us. Our plan of action had always worked.

I was on my own this time. After a good burst of running ahead, I looked back to check for their flashlights. While I could see tiny bursts of light, I was almost far enough ahead that I'd be able to sneak off-trail. I began sprinting in long bounds to put even more space between us. They still called out my name but were beginning to sound farther away. After my burst of speed, I could barely hear them, so I took the opportunity and abandoned the footpath, carefully creeping away from the creek and deeper into the woods. I did my best to step quietly. I crawled over logs and squeezed through tight spaces between trees and bushes before finally decided on a particularly dense thicket of trees.

I paused before climbing one of the trees to listen for the cops. I could hear their voices again. I climbed up as carefully as I could, making sure to leave space for my backpack to make it through and, once I was high enough, sat and focused on slowing my breath.

"Izzie! We know you're out here!" They were nearing the part of the footpath where I'd crept off into untamed woods. Now I could hear their footsteps. I could see bright beams of their flashlights shining through the trees. I closed my eyes. I was far enough off the path that they probably wouldn't be able to see me hiding, but if the flattened grass gave my path away, they might wander toward me—and then I'd be screwed.

But their footsteps began to fade; they continued farther down the footpath. I opened my eyes. From the way they were swinging their flashlights, I could tell that they were doing more scanning than clue-hunting. As their voices became distant again, I let out a sigh of relief. I moved around delicately on the tree branch for comfort. At some point, they'd turn around and retrace their steps, so I needed to stay put.

"Your parents are worried about you, Izzie," I heard far in the distance. "They just want you safe."

I began to nod off. The branch was sturdy, my head heavy against the trunk. Though I was tired, I kept willing myself to stay awake. But it got harder by the minute. The cool night's breeze fluttered through my hair. I promised myself I'd only close my eyes for a moment.

I jerked awake when their voices, distant only a moment ago, startled me with their clarity and proximity. "Izzie! Come on!" They must have turned around. They sounded really close.

When I instinctively looked around again for their flashlights, I found them immediately. They were standing at the place on the footpath where I'd taken off into the woods. I heard the murmured baritones of them talking to each other but couldn't tell what they were saying.

Then I heard snapping, breaking branches—the movement of men walking through the brush. It was over. I closed my eyes and hoped for the best. As it turned out, hoping didn't help much. They found me.

They lectured me on the way back to our cars. I scowled at them, staying silent as they put me in the back seat. We left my car out there. I was fuming the whole way home as they attempted to try and get me to talk about why I hadn't told anyone where I was going.

My parents talked to them for a while after they'd delivered me back home, thanking them and apologizing for my behavior. But I went straight to my room without looking at either of my parents and blockaded the door with my desk chair. All I'd wanted was peace and quiet.

CHAPTER 4

MATT COMES HOME

———

After the cop fiasco, the entire house began to feel like an interrogation room I couldn't escape. My parents pried into why I would run away, what I would be doing post-graduation, and if I wanted to talk about my moods. Would a counselor help? A doctor visit? Summer camp? Antidepressants?

"We're just concerned about you," my mom said, but I only shrugged.

"Welcome to the party," I replied.

I spent the remaining weeks of senior year doodling off-centered patterns in my notebooks, eating silently at dinner, and generally sulking. I wasn't sure how to loop my parents into the way I was feeling without pointing out that at least *some* of the blame lay with them. Like the blur of a videotape being fast-forwarded, I didn't take in much of the remaining moments of high school. I felt that I was cheating myself of an important moment in my life—a moment that was probably critical to the overall plot of my story. But I didn't have much control over the rapid pace of everything. I wasn't the one with the remote control, and nothing happened when I shook my fist at the sky in the desperate hope that maybe God might smite me and put me out of my misery.

It wasn't as though I holed up and isolated myself, though. I was going to more parties than I ever had before with my classmates. Maybe it was because we had known each other all our lives, but the mere thought of saying goodbye after graduation and leaving for college, setting off for new adventures, seemed to bond us all even closer in the last legs of our senior year.

Every single weekend, I was out on the town, drinking shitty Oklahoma beer from the state line with my peers as we tried to cram in as much excitement as possible.

"Can you believe it? We finally made it. I'm getting out of this town as fast as I can," my best friend Heather said one night. I nodded at her and attempted a smile, but I couldn't stop thinking about how uncertain my own future was turning out to be. Doing my best to ignore these fears, I kept on drinking.

For all the excitement of partying every weekend, getting ready for graduation, and picking out a dress for prom— which I may have puked all over at the after-party—I felt empty and lost. My friends seemed to be drinking in celebration of finishing high school and planning the rest of their lives. But the more I drank, the more I wanted to quietly slip away into the fuzzy black space of wordlessness in my head. Soon, I was stumbling home every weekend and even some weekdays to fall drunkenly into my bed and welcome dark and dreamless sleep. Jealously, I listened to my peers talk about the universities they would be attending, the careers they would be pursuing, and the dreams they would be chasing. I'd nod and wonder where in the world *I* might belong.

One night, I expressed some of these fears to Heather, who I'd known since kindergarten. It was about three in the morning, and we were parked out on a dusty farm road with enough beer stacked in the backseat to make us sick.

"I just don't know what I'm going to do after graduation," I told her. She was sitting in the driver's seat, knees tucked up against the steering wheel.

"What are you talking about? Weren't you talking about going to the same school as Matt?" She took a drink.

"I don't know. We're in a weird place right now. But if I go to school, what do I study? What am I good at?"

"Are you serious right now?" she asked, and I paused. How was I supposed to explain that I felt like a nobody with no destiny, a person all alone in the world with no footsteps to follow?

I shrugged at her, rolled down the window, and lit up a cigarette. "I just mean, I don't know who I'm supposed to be. I know I want to do *something*, I just don't know what. And I don't want to spend my life following Matt around."

"You won't. I wouldn't worry about Matt if I were you. You've been fine this year without him. But if you're worried about what you're good at, you should write about it," she said, blue eyes twinkling in the moonlight.

"Yeah," I said, thoughtfully. "Maybe."

"No, really," she said. "You need to be writing. That's where you're going. You're a writer, Iz."

"You're nuts," I laughed. But despite my drunkenness, I thought, quite lucidly in fact, that writing really was the one thing that made me feel truly free. That is, when I was brave enough to put the words on the page and face them—something that hadn't happened since my birthday.

But despite her consolation that I didn't need Matt and her encouragement toward writing, I still drank away the anxieties that remained. I didn't know how I felt about Matt, and I definitely didn't feel confident about my writing. But no matter how I tried to drown those things in booze, that one conversation remained with me.

As the semester came to a close, I felt more and more hopeless with each day that passed. I didn't belong in this town, I didn't feel like I belonged with my family, and my future was still unwritten. Though I thought often of the confidence with which Heather had told me I was a writer, that particular path seemed too big a dream to chase, especially since my writing had been completely absent lately.

As I thought about all four of my parents—two who had quietly loved me and tried their best to raise me to be a sweetly obedient girl, one who had fallen into drugs and struggled with mental illness, and the last one, a complete mystery—I wondered how I was like any of them. How was I supposed to know what to do with my life? At least I knew what I *didn't* want to do, I thought, but even that contributed to an ever-dizzying lack of direction.

I began to call Matt every day in hopes that he would pick up his phone, even if it was just to shut me up and tell me he was busy. I began to worry that, despite the letter he had sent me, something had gone wrong. I wondered if he enjoyed the space away from me. The voicemails I left quickly became shorter and more urgent. I began writing long emails in hopes that he would respond sooner, but he never did. I was on my own and worried that when he came home, it would be to tell me something I didn't want to hear. By the last week of school, I had given up completely. Who needed him? Maybe Heather was right. I had other things to figure out.

Matt didn't specify what day he would be home in his letter. He seemed to think it was fun to surprise me. I usually enjoyed surprises, but graduation was looming, my parents were watching me anxiously as if I'd sprouted antlers, and the general nervousness I had about the rest of my life was consuming me. I really just wanted him home as soon as possible so I could scream at him for not taking the time to answer my phone calls and emails. A couple of weeks might have been excusable, but it had been a month and a half since my birthday, and all I'd received was one stupid letter and a stream of pathetic voicemails. I thought about writing to tell him not to come, maybe even leaving a voicemail saying as much, but I kept chickening out. I didn't want to go through all of this alone anymore.

By the time he finally made his reappearance, it was the week before graduation. It was a Friday night, and I was up late sorting through the things I would take with me once I figured out where to go. Though I'd been accepted at a few colleges, I still hadn't made any big decisions. I wasn't even sure I wanted to go to school. The only thing I was sure of was that I would be moving out. I needed my own space.

But with so many decisions still to make, I wasn't very motivated while poking through the things in my room. I was sitting on my bed flipping through an old journal from junior high when I heard our dog, Shadow, running toward the fence outside my window. Then came a soft thud of feet landing on the ground. Matt's voice rumbled gently outside in the yard; he greeted the dog and headed toward my window. I looked around my room hopelessly. It was a wreck. I should have cleaned. But he should have called.

When he tapped on the window, I pulled the blinds up and opened the window. He and the dog both climbed in. While the dog nestled into my unmade bed to enjoy this rare opportunity to sleep in the house, Matt grabbed me by the hips and kissed me. Immediately, I slapped him across the face as hard as I could.

"What's *wrong* with you?" I asked, disgusted.

He stepped back, a look of calm surprise on his face, then closed the window behind him but left the blinds up. He looked around my room as I glared at him.

"I know it must look like a fucking pigsty in here, but I've been too upset to clean," I said flatly.

He frowned at me. "You know I don't care about the mess. And you know that actual pigs are pretty clean." He paused with half a grin, but upon realizing that I wasn't going to laugh at his remark, said, "I deserved that, but I'm worried about you. Come here."

He pulled me close and hugged me tight.

"No!" I pulled away from him. "I've called and emailed you! What the hell?"

"I know," he said.

"You *know*?"

"Let's go to the lake," he said.

I looked at the dog, snuggled in and already asleep in my bed. I wanted so much to join him rather than deal with my jerk of a boyfriend who thought he could just ignore me and show up out of the blue.

"Yeah," I said sarcastically. "We should go to the lake. You can tell me all about why you've been ignoring my calls and emails."

"I was busy, and I was scared I wouldn't know what to say to you," he said sheepishly, ears turning pink. "I wanted to see you in person so we could talk about everything that's been going on with you. I know I should have called or emailed, and I'm sorry." He gave me puppy eyes. "Let's go skinny-dipping. Tonight is the perfect night for it."

"That's some shit, and you know it." I sat back down on my bed and closed the journal I'd been thumbing through.

He moved to sit next to me, but before he could, I held out my arm.

"Nope, no, sir. You want to try that apology again?" I challenged. I couldn't believe him. What was he thinking? His excuses fell flat.

"Baby, I'm sorry. I really am. Nothing I could have said in a letter or email would have helped."

I held steady in my hateful gaze toward him. If I stayed silent, he would crack. He always did.

"And you know I tried to call! I left you so many voice-mails," he pleaded and moved toward me again. I put my arm down, letting him sit on the edge of the bed.

"Whatever." I didn't know what else to say. I was angry to be abandoned for so long, but also emotionally drained. And he was the only person I could think of who would listen to me patiently as I worked through things out loud. He offered a sad little smile.

"Forgive me? The semester is over, and you have me home for the whole summer," he said in a small voice. "We never have to be apart again, I promise."

I rolled my eyes at him. After all this time, he thought he could waltz in here like nothing had happened.

"You can be mad at me all you want." He smiled again softly. "I deserve it."

He scooted closer to me as I eyed him warily, then said, "But I also know how to cheer you up. I brought your favorite beer. We could go drink it at the lake." He gave me a cheesy grin.

Despite myself, I cracked half a smile. I was mad, but as I looked at his muted green eyes I realized—with an unfamiliar twinge of something that felt like desperation, apathy, and a hint of happiness—that I needed him. I'd spent the last two months needing him and, my anger aside, he was the only one in the world I felt comfortable telling the truth to. The energy it took to remain angry with him was too much to hold onto, so I sighed and let it slip out of my body to make room for the original feeling of needing him to comfort me.

"I assumed you'd want to go to the lake the minute you got back," I finally said and reached out to pat his arm.

"So. Skinny-dipping? And once we're all tired, we can drink beer and lay on top of the car and look at the stars. What d'ya say? All in favor say aye?" His eyes twinkled.

"Aye," I said, trying not to laugh. "You asshole."

"The ayes have it!"

I pulled my car keys out from under my pillow and handed them over. "You drive."

He took the keys and went toward the window to open it again. I followed him out, leaving the dog behind to enjoy his sleep.

* * *

Somehow, being in the passenger seat as he drove with his left hand on the steering wheel and right hand on my thigh, I finally felt like maybe things *would* turn out okay.

It had been strange to be away from him for a year. I missed him being around. Talking on the phone, emailing, or writing letters didn't fill the gap. And the silence between us since my birthday was the longest stretch yet, with only one letter each way to prove that we still thought about each other.

Though I was still upset that he had left me in the lurch at the worst possible time, I could feel myself beginning to relax now that we were back together. And for all those missed phone calls and unanswered emails? I had all summer to give him hell for being such a jerk.

Once we reached a good swimming spot down the creek, we stripped naked, gave each other sly once-overs, and waded in.

"The water's perfect," I sighed. Once the water was up to my belly button, I stretched out my arms and fell backward into the water. I heard him splash after me right before he grabbed my toes and I had to surface quickly just to shriek.

"Come on," I directed. "Let's swim up the creek a ways."

"Tell me a story," he said suddenly as we both fell into a lazy side stroke. "I've had enough of the world, and I want a story. Ridiculous as possible, please."

I grinned. This was one of my favorite games. Although I dabbled often in poetry and diary entries, what I really wanted to do was write stories. Weird ones. I didn't know if they'd ever sell big, but who really cared about that? It would be pretty cool to hold my own book.

I turned over to float and think up a ridiculous story on the spot.

"Once upon a time," I began. "There was a girl who believed all the wild stories her grandmother told her. Everybody else thought the grandmother had lost her mind."

I looked over to find him looking at me with a face that reminded me of the awestruck way he looked at me when he'd first asked me out on a date. I ignored his attempt at being cute and continued.

"The grandmother told her that she once met a unicorn and a mermaid and knew where some of their magic was buried. 'If you find it,' she told the girl, 'you'll have magic nobody else possesses. I was the last of humankind to know about it.'"

"Unicorns and mermaids, huh?" he chuckled.

"Yep," I said. "So, the granddaughter went into the forest where her grandmother told her to go, started digging and, sure enough, there was a unicorn horn and mermaid scales. But something went wrong. Her wish to know everything was too powerful, and she gained the Sight."

"The Sight?"

"Like, a seer. Or a fortune-teller. She could see the future."

"Oh, right. Okay. Then what?"

"Well, then, she suddenly knew how and when her grandmother would die, of course, so she raced back as fast as she could, but…"

"But?"

"But even though she was given the Sight, it turned out to be more of a curse than a blessing. Her grandmother was dead before she got there."

"Oh, it's got a moral and everything. You're good." He laughed. "One of these days, I'm going to make you sit down and type up all the stories you tell me *and* all the stories in your notebooks."

"I haven't really written that much lately, to be honest. I don't know where to start." The words fell out of my mouth carelessly, and I didn't realize how much it upset me that I hadn't written until I saw his eyebrows raise. I slipped under the water and swam back upstream to where we'd left our stuff to avoid the inevitable question of *why* I hadn't written. When I popped out of the water behind him, I yelled, "Come on!"

Once he'd caught up and followed me back to shore, we curled up in oversized towels and sat down on the log that overlooked the creek. I opened my half-empty pack of cigarettes and lit one up while he cracked open the two large beers he'd snuck into my car.

After a moment or two of silence, he turned to me seriously. "You want to tell me what's on your mind?"

"Yeah," I said, "It's just that I don't know where to start. I mean, I've missed you, but I don't want to ruin tonight."

"You won't ruin anything. I want to know what you're thinking. That letter you sent me was quite the work of art."

I laughed weakly. "Yeah. I know. I just don't know how to go through all of what I'm going through. Like I don't know how to do it alone, but I also don't want to burden you with it, either. I feel like I'm drowning. But just because I'm drowning doesn't mean I should pull you down with me, you know?"

He didn't say anything. He just looked at me with those bright green eyes and waited.

"So," I said, blowing smoke out my nostrils. "There's a bunch of paperwork that I've been digging through. I've already organized it, scrapbooked it, and memorized it, and I don't really know what else to do with it. But it's there. And I've got this locket." I touched the piece of jewelry around my neck. I wondered suddenly if it was safe to take it swimming with me. "My parents have been silent. The whole house has been weird. Even Ronnie is acting weird."

"Even Ronnie?"

"Yeah. I think maybe she doesn't want to be in the middle of it, but I kind of think that she might feel jaded, too. Don't you think there's some big mysterious folder about her adoption somewhere, too?"

"Yeah. That's weird. Then again, Ronnie isn't like you."

"Yeah," I said.

"Okay," he said slowly, dragging the word out as he lined up his thoughts. "So, you have all of this paperwork, and you don't know what to do with it. Is it too much information? Or is it not enough?"

I looked at him blankly.

"I just mean, you've always been pretty curious about your background and what makes you the way you are. Does the paperwork answer your questions?"

I took a long drag of my cigarette and looked out across the creek as I pondered the question.

"No," I said finally. "It's a lot of information, so in some ways, it's overwhelming to take in. But I think what frustrates me the most is that I somehow have even more questions than I started with."

He drank his beer; I followed suit. For once, I wasn't sure I was following his line of thinking. But, I had to remind myself, I didn't remember much of what I wrote to him in that letter. He was probably trying to piece together the panic he saw there and the confusion he was seeing now in person. He wouldn't have to be catching up on all this if he'd just answered my phone calls or emails, though, I thought angrily.

"I think what we do is go to the adoption agency and demand more information, see if we can find your birthmother," he said.

"Well," I said. "There was one form called Vital Statistic or something. I filled it out to request information from the state about my adoption. I already mailed it off. Maybe it takes them a while."

"Maybe," he mused. "But the state wouldn't have much. Maybe a birth certificate. The agency would have full records."

He had a point. I'd spent almost two months wallowing in self-pity, but my pity party had blinded me to the ways in which I could seek new information. Maybe the agency would have that information. Maybe I could find my birthmother. But my pity party hadn't blinded me to the fact that Matt had been gone for this entire saga.

I kissed him, then pinched his arm hard.

"Ow! Do I hear a road trip in our near future?"

"You would really do that? Come with me and all? To look for my birthmother? You sure you can handle being around me that much? After ignoring me for so long?"

"Don't be stupid. Of course, I would. Are we going?"

"We're going. After I graduate next weekend, we'll go."

I took one last swig of beer and put out my cigarette, then looked at him sternly.

"But I'm not being stupid," I said. "Let's go home."

"Only if you don't pinch me anymore."

"No promises. You know you're in trouble." I pinched him again, this time even harder, and laughed as he winced.

We didn't say a word the whole drive home, his hand in mine and rock music keeping us awake. There was nothing I could say that wouldn't start a fight, and I didn't have the emotional capacity to get into an argument with the one person in the world who might understand me best. The last year had been difficult. The last two months had been the worst of it. And with him back home so suddenly after such a long period of silence, I felt as though I was holding hands with a stranger. I couldn't shake my irritation with him, especially when I thought about the pathetic apology he'd given me. But I didn't know what else to do except try to believe that, in time, everything between us would return to normal. I couldn't throw a five-year relationship away for two months of missed phone calls, could I?

And as for the upcoming plan to look for my birth-mother—or at least see what information we could find—I wasn't worried about what I would tell my parents. Maybe they'd understand. Maybe they wouldn't. I was going to go, either way.

CHAPTER 5

THE ROAD TRIP

Matt and I set out on our journey to the adoption agency the morning after my graduation in hopes of finding out more about my birthmother. I was hopeful we might even find her. Begrudgingly, I had informed my parents early on graduation morning that I would be gone for a while, but they could call me. I didn't want them to send the Texas Rangers after us. I told them I'd be going to the after-parties following the graduation ceremony, then Matt and I would be driving straight to the adoption agency the next morning to look for information. My parents wearily accepted this plan, and neither seemed interested in fighting about it.

It was a good thing I'd packed everything ahead of time. The graduation parties didn't end until about four in the morning, and I was supposed to be on my porch waiting for Matt to come get me by seven. In a moment of drunken genius when I arrived home from the parties, I decided to drag all my stuff for the trip outside and slept for three glorious hours on the front patio swinging bench.

When I heard Matt's truck pull up, I mustered the energy to get up and gather my things. I still felt a little dizzy even after my death nap. I threw my duffel bag in the back and put my backpack on the floorboard of the passenger seat with me before climbing up into the truck. Once there, I immediately dragged a blanket out from the back seat to sleep with.

"Hey, sleepy," he yawned. We obviously hadn't planned this trip very well. What were we thinking, trying to leave so early the morning after so much partying?

"Can I take a nap?"

"Yeah, I guess."

"You won't fall asleep at the wheel and kill us?"

"If I do, I'll make sure we both go quick."

"Okay." I leaned over the console to kiss him. He reached for the stereo, turning on some music. "You're going to have to deal with my loud music because I have to stay awake," he warned.

I shrugged and fell asleep before we'd even hit the highway out of town.

When I woke up, we had just reached Shamrock's city limits, and scenes from a strange dream were still shifting through my mind's eye: a shimmery blue mermaid tail splashing in the lake, her long silver hair, and... a cave full of clams? I pondered these images for a moment until my stomach rumbled.

"Hey, look. A McDonald's. Let's get something to eat," I said, seeing an exit sign with those famous golden arches. Matt agreed and pulled off the highway.

He picked out a sunny corner of the dining area, and soon I was feeling much more awake.

"I had this weird dream," I said, sliding into the booth. "Want to play?"

"Sure." He grinned. "Dream interpreter at your service."

"Awesome. Okay, so I was on this island, and I got in the water to explore. Then I found an underwater cave beneath the island. And in the cave was this little cove where sunshine beamed through, and an ancient mermaid sat on a rock in the light."

"An *ancient* mermaid?"

"Like a bunch of wrinkles and silver hair, you know. She was old."

"That's weird."

"Yeah, and she invited me to slurp clams with her while she told stories. I'm trying to remember..." What was one of the stories she was talking about? There was the sunshine on the rocks and the clams and then...

"Oh!" I exclaimed. "One of them was about how important gardens are for communities."

"A mermaid concerned about gardening?"

"Yeah, I don't know. Anyway. At the end of the dream, she told me she had a present for me and gave me a necklace." Then I reached down and pulled out my golden locket for emphasis. "It was *this* necklace."

"Whoa," he said, laughing. By that time, our breakfast had arrived, so we chowed down.

"What if your birthmother is actually a mermaid and gave you up because you came out human?" he asked.

I rolled my eyes. "Dude. How would I even exist? Human-mermaid sex wouldn't work."

"Fine, fine. What's *your* interpretation of the dream?"

I paused to finish chewing. "Maybe I'm worried I have to find my birthmother before she's old? Since that mermaid is old and she had stories to tell, right? And that's what I'm looking for: the stories. And maybe the cave is a kind of jail?"

He lifted an eyebrow at me, then asked, "What's with the cave being a jail?"

"Maybe..." I searched my thoughts for a moment but came up blank. "I don't really know where that one came from."

We ate the rest of our breakfast in silence, but I took the time to look at Matt's face in the sunshine. His mess of shaggy, light brown hair and those bright green eyes felt like home. And yet, something was off this time. He wasn't as playful as he usually was during our past dream interpretation games. But then again, he might have been hungover.

"Hit the road?" I asked once we'd finished eating.

"Let's go," he said and handed me the keys to the truck. My turn to drive.

I pulled out of the McDonalds' parking lot and steered us southbound. As I hit the highway and began to fiddle with the radio dials, he finally spoke up.

"Are you nervous?"

Startled, I looked at him and then out the window at the sprawl of open land before answering. "I mean... yeah. I'm terrified. What if she's everything I think she is? A drug addict, a crazy person? And worse, what if she's nothing like I think she is? What if my creativity, my charm, my brains come from her and we become best friends? I'm terrified that I won't know who I am if we don't find her. And . . . I'm terrified I won't know who I am if we *do*."

After a moment of silence, Matt said, "Izzie. Even if you don't know who you are, I do. We're going to find her, and you'll get the answers to all your questions."

I gave him a dubious look.

"You know," he said slowly. "That's a good idea. Questions. Write some questions down so you'll know what you want to say when we do find her." He reached into the backseat to dig through his backpack. He then handed me two handmade journals—the ones he'd told me about in his letter.

"But I'm driving!" I laughed. "I can't write right now!"

"Sure ya can." He grinned. "There's nobody out on these highways. Just drive with your knee."

Laughing, I flipped a journal open to the first page and smiled. Maybe it *would* help to write out some questions. I propped my leg up to hold the steering wheel steady with my knee, put the journal on the wheel, and began writing. Matt quickly fell asleep in the passenger seat as I did my best to keep the truck at seventy-five miles an hour and in between the faded road lines.

By the time we hit Childress, I had about ten decent questions written out. But more ideas were bubbling in my head. I'd have to get Matt to drive to really dig into the rest of them.

I pulled into a gas station and kissed him on the head to wake him up before going inside to stock up on snacks and pay for gas.

When I got back out to the car, Matt was just opening the door to get out. Before he could, I dumped the bag of snacks in his lap.

"Good morning, sunshine!" I beamed at him. "It's your turn to drive. I have so many things I need to write and get out of my head. You were right. The questions helped!"

"Wait," he said. "I need coffee."

I laughed and pointed him toward the gas station. He ambled off while I turned to fill up the truck. Leaving the truck to fill, I crawled into the passenger seat and began outlining my thoughts. The questions themselves were important, but I also wanted the outline to be sturdy. I was going to write a book.

* * *

By the time we'd reached Abilene to stop off for lunch, I had the whole book planned out. In three rotating narratives, I would simultaneously document the lives of my parents, my birthmother, and myself. All the perspectives in one place. When Matt asked me how I'd do it, I explained that I would begin by working backward. First, I'd list out the scenes that I wanted, then formulate the questions I'd need to get there. I wanted childhood histories, romantic scenes, struggles, fears, and all the rest. My questions would demand answers.

Matt, though obviously intrigued by my idea, played devil's advocate. "What if your parents are uncomfortable answering these questions?"

"Don't underestimate the long-ignored ego," I said as I drew boxes that indicated the three different story outlines.

"Yeah, but are you going to tell the truth about what happened with your parents? Won't that just make tension rise? And what about your birthmother? You don't know if she'll want to be in your book."

"Everyone likes to be listened to," I snapped. "And everyone should be able to tell their story." I glared at him. Devil's advocate was one thing. But he was flirting with crossing that line. I waited until I held his gaze. "If they don't tell their stories to me, how am I supposed to tell mine?"

"Yeah," he said quickly. "I'm just worried about what happens if they tell you something you don't want to hear."

I raised my eyebrows at him in defiance, then grinned. "Nobody tells me no."

He laughed loudly. "Yeah, no shit. But…" He paused and let the grin slide off his face. "What happens after you write the book?"

"What do you mean?"

He shrugged. "School? Job? Gap year?"

I shook my head. "I don't know. I don't think I'll know until I can piece this story together."

"Well," he said. "I was thinking you could come live with me. Assuming you want to go to the same school, or even if you just want a little time to keep thinking."

Surprised by this, I didn't have a response right away. I hadn't even begun to think about anything like that—not seriously anyway.

"I don't know." I shook my head.

"I don't want to be without you another year," he said, reaching over to squeeze my thigh.

I gave him a small smile and looked out the window. Though I'd been so upset with him for not responding for so long, I wondered if maybe I preferred the distance after all. At least with him gone, I had time to myself to brood. He was supporting my quest for knowledge, but maybe this was the kind of thing I was supposed to do on my own.

For the rest of the day, I cycled between writing, planning, and bouncing ideas off Matt. Silence fell over us in intervals, and though he often reached over to pat my thigh or hold my hand, I focused on my outline. Whether I liked to admit that he was right or not, I really *didn't* know what we would find or what would happen after, and I wasn't ready to look that far ahead.

We got to San Antonio after the adoption agency's closing hours, so we picked up some food and headed straight to a motel. Finally, with no more driving to do and my hand aching from writing so much over an eight-hour drive, we ate dinner on the bed and fell asleep with half-eaten cheese-burgers left out on the side table.

CHAPTER 6

STEALING HOPE

———

When I woke up, the digital clock said it was almost three in the morning. I was hot and sweaty. Another dream had taken me someplace strange, but all I could remember was that in it I'd ridden on the back of a giant bird. I looked over at Matt beside me; he had apparently stripped down at some point. He was fast asleep and sprawled out. I swung my legs over the side of the bed and stripped as I walked toward the window to crack it open. When I crawled back in bed, he stirred as I folded my body into his. He was cooler than me and wiggled toward me in his sleep.

A train whistled in the distance, and the slightest breeze came in through the cracked window. I closed my eyes and tried to find sleep again but couldn't. My mind was completely awake. The adoption agency wouldn't be open for another five or six hours. I knew I needed to get some sleep, but it was like being awake on Christmas Eve. Except I wasn't sure what I'd find in the morning. Maybe everything I'd ever wanted. Maybe not.

I dangled my hand over the side of the bed and played with the shadows my fingers made on the floor from the dim city light filtering in through the curtains. I already missed the deep darkness of night only possible in a small town. Swinging my hand back and forth, I put myself into an uneasy sleep.

Sometime after this, I felt Matt's cool skin on my back. When his hand came to rest on my stomach, I couldn't help but wiggle backward to move closer. Once settled, I closed my eyes again and sighed.

He moved the hair off my neck and kissed it. "Hey," he whispered. I murmured back. I let go of the breath I found myself holding from the goosebumps he'd given me. He moved his hand upward from my stomach, and I arched my back to meet the rest of him behind me as he gently squeezed.

"Don't you say a word," he whispered, and I rolled over to face him. His eyes were deep green now, like a dark forest in the moonlight. He pulled me closer, and our legs twisted together as we figured each other out, all over again.

Like an animal starved, I kissed him hard and drank up the taste of a nineteen-year-old who'd just yesterday been my fourteen-year-old boyfriend sneaking me out at night to swing at the park. There, we'd talk about all the plans we had for our lives. So much had changed and yet somehow between us, everything was the same. Feeling his skin against mine all but burst my soul open.

"Where have you been?" I whispered. "It's been…"

"Shhh," he said and worshipped my body with strong hands until I couldn't handle it. I climbed on top and held his hands in mine above his head.

"You're mine," I said, kissing him.

"No. You're mine," he said. Moving like two torrential tornadoes dead set on destruction, our bodies tangled and tore at each other as the heat of passion overtook us.

We poured wordless love into one another until our bodies lay shaking in the sweaty aftermath in a heap on the bed.

"I love you," I laughed.

"I know." He grinned, and he laid on his back to breathe. "Go to sleep, babe."

I put my head on his chest and fell into sleep without dreams—warm, content, and safe.

* * *

In the morning, we shared a shower. I felt like a stranger intruding on a private moment; he had gained a little beer belly while away, and I found it strange to see such a difference in a body I once had memorized. On the way out of the hotel, we both took a free cup of coffee from the breakfast nook. Once we got in the truck, I lit up a cigarette.

"So," he said as he got in behind the wheel.

"Yep," I said.

I had loaded a day backpack with some water bottles, both our wallets, the binder of scrapbooked paperwork, and the journals he'd given me.

We navigated through San Antonio until we came to a little place that, though in the middle of housing neighborhoods and just off to the side of a commercial street, looked like a little farming village. Several different buildings sat atop a large spread of land that boasted tall trees and a large garden. A few of the buildings looked like old dormitory apartments, and we parked at the one with a sign that read: *Welcome Center.*

The whole place looked like it hadn't been redecorated since the 1980s. Taking a deep breath, I got out of the car and stood on the steps. Matt followed close behind. He put his hand in mine, and we walked in the front door.

The woman behind the desk had blond hair that, with the help of a ton of hairspray, fell voluminously to her shoulders. Her lipstick was so red it looked as though she'd gulped down blood for breakfast. The crow's feet at the edges of her eyes crinkled as she smiled at us.

"Good morning! How can I help y'all?"

"I'm looking for some information," I offered.

"Sure," she said and began piling pamphlets on the counter. *Why You Should Consider Adoption, Adopting with Us,* and other titles came up.

"You two looking to adopt a baby?"

Matt recoiled behind me, but I smiled politely. "Uh no, actually, I'm here to look up some information about my birthmother and my own adoption. I just turned eighteen," I said.

"Oh, honey," she responded. "There's not much I can help you with there. Do you have any documentation?"

"Yeah, actually. Yes." I dumped my backpack on the counter and dug out the binder full of carefully organized documents. "Is there anything particular you need?"

"Well. We keep records of case numbers, but the state holds those records. You need to go to court if it's your birth certificate you're wanting. Usually, we only keep track of addresses."

"Addresses because all correspondence has to come through you?"

"That's right, honey. But I can't give that kind of thing out. It's confidential. You and your birthmother would both have to consent in writing to give out last names and addresses and all."

"I see."

"Here." She handed me a paper. "I've got a form you can fill out to consent to sharing your last name and address. Since I've got the information in the computer, I can mail the same form to your birthmother as well. I'll look up her information here in a second, if you think that's something you'd like to do." I nodded, so she continued, "If she sends it back signed, I can mail you the information. Then you'll be free to communicate freely, so long as you both attend a short course."

"A course?"

"It's short, honey. It's just an overview of things to look out for when meeting a new relative. Once both of you consent, we send out the information about it." She smiled.

I looked the form over and began filling it out while she typed some things into the computer. Just as she began to scroll through the page on her monitor, a phone rang somewhere down the hall behind her.

"Whoops," she laughed. "I'll be right back, excuse me."

Matt didn't waste a second. The moment she left, he reached over the counter and looked at the screen.

"Write this down," he said, and I quickly turned over one of the pamphlets still left on the counter and waited, pen in hand.

"Carole Anne Wilson," he read. "Last known address. There's three, get ready."

"Wilson," I repeated as I wrote. It was strange to suddenly know her last name after a lifetime of only knowing her as Carole Anne.

He dictated the addresses, and I quickly wrote them down. I could hear the lady talking on the phone in the distance. I wasn't sure how much time we had.

"There's a couple phone numbers, too," he said. We managed to get the first one down before hearing the receptionist's footsteps coming back toward us. I slipped the pamphlet into my pocket and continued to fill out the form she'd left me with. As she entered the room, Matt winked at me.

"Here," I said as I slid the completed form across the counter to her, smiling.

"Oh, perfect! Yes, I'll get this filed away. Can you verify that this is your correct address?" She turned the monitor around and I looked. On the screen were my parents' names, mine, our address, and home phone number.

"Yep," I said. "That's right. Is there anything else you can help me with? This is all new to me, so any little bit helps."

"That's about it, sweetie. You can fill out this form," she pulled a Vital Statistic form out from under the counter, "if you want the legal records, but you've got to have a good reason."

"Oh, I've already sent that off," I said. "Is it usually difficult to get documents from the state?"

"Yes, unfortunately," she sighed. "You might want to ask one of our lawyers around here about that process. I think one of them should be in later this afternoon if you want to stick around?"

I looked at Matt, who shrugged.

I thought about it for a moment before shaking my head. "No, I think I'll just wait for the communication stuff to come through. I'd really like to meet her."

She nodded at me.

"But is there any way you could give me a name and phone number for one of your lawyers in case I want to call back later?" I asked.

"Of course, sugar, let me go grab a card for ya." She got up again and disappeared down the hall.

"I say we go find these addresses and see what shows up," Matt said to me under his breath as soon as the receptionist was out of hearing range.

"I agree. More road tripping for us, eh?"

She returned with a business card and handed it to me.

"Thank you so much for all your help," I said, putting the card in my pocket along with the pamphlet with all the addresses.

She smiled. "Of course. Y'all have a good day now."

Feeling optimistic, I followed Matt back out to the truck and got in. It looked like we'd be driving for the rest of the day. All three addresses were in Albuquerque, New Mexico. It was barely past nine in the morning, so if we booked it, we could maybe hit town before the night got too late. I hadn't let go of the anxiety about whether we'd find Carole or not. But Matt was happy, and I found myself believing—almost desperately—that I might really meet my birthmother and get to ask the big questions about her life.

CHAPTER 7

THE CLUES CONTINUE

———

It was a good day to be on the road. We got some cheap burritos at a gas station on the way out of town and asked the clerk if he could tell us which road led to Albuquerque. Though he didn't have a map to add to our Texas map, he did tell us to follow US-87 toward San Angelo.

The sun was bright, the shuffle feature on the iPod played all the right tunes, and I felt especially optimistic.

"I didn't really expect it to be that easy," Matt told me as he drove us out of town.

I reached over to squeeze his thigh. "It's because of your quick thinking." I grinned.

"Yes, well, I can be useful sometimes. How will you ever pay me back?" He smiled at me.

I laughed. "I don't know what you're expecting. A prize? I'm going to work on my book for the next bout of driving." I reached for my backpack on the floorboard by my feet.

"Not all of it," he said. "You're gonna have to drive some, too."

I pulled out my journal and a pen. On the first several pages, I'd written out questions for all three parents to help me piece together their stories. On the next several pages were three columns that followed each narrative. With my parents and my birthmother, I thought I would detail their own childhoods in summary form before dropping into the romances that led to me. And, of course, my story would begin at my birth and end with turning eighteen.

Matt had claimed my book was terribly ambitious, and I was beginning to think he was right. Even so, I couldn't help but think that—beyond giving readers a glimpse into all three sides of an adoption story—it would also give me a sense of peace. If I could somehow wrap up the past, it might be easier for me to navigate the future.

As he drove, I copied down the three addresses and phone number into my journal and began detailing my experience so far in narrative style. The difficult part would be summing up my entire childhood and adolescence in a way that clearly laid out what had happened and how I felt but also portrayed my parents as acting through love. Though they'd made mistakes, as all parents do, and I was rightfully upset with them, I could still recognize that they loved me. Their love was a deep, quiet thing that I didn't understand most of the time. But it was still there, unwaveringly steady. It would be a hard line to balance.

Starting the story, it turned out, was pretty difficult. I went through an entire page and a half of first sentences before I came to one that sounded right.

"How's this?" I asked Matt a couple of hours later, holding up my notebook to read aloud. "Once upon a time, my parents told me, a woman in San Antonio got pregnant." I looked at him expectantly.

"It sounds like the beginning to a fairy tale," he said thoughtfully. "Is your life a fairytale?"

"I think I'm going to make it sound like one, then smash it to pieces by the end of the first chapter. What do you think?"

He laughed. "I have no idea. It's your book."

Smiling, I put the notebook back in my lap and did my best to write the first chapter. For such a short thing, it took me another two hours to write, and by that time, we'd hit Big Spring.

At the gas station, we asked for directions again. This time, we celebrated our luck when the cashier handed us a map to New Mexico. We charted the rest of our course while Matt filled up the truck with gas.

"You drive?" he said to me as we stood against the truck stretching our legs.

"That's good with me."

With the romantic beat of summer love songs from the 1990s playing, Matt decorated the margins of my journal pages, and I daydreamed about what it might be like to meet my birthmother. San Antonio to Albuquerque turned out to be a much longer drive than the Texas panhandle to San Antonio, but we made it just after dark. There we found a little motel on the edge of town to stay in for the night.

When Matt crawled into bed beside me, I curled up inside his arms and whispered, "Thank you for coming with me."

"Anything for you, babe," he said, and we both fell asleep, exhausted from the day's long drive.

* * *

The minute I woke up in the morning, I was ready to go. My nerves were completely on edge about what the day might hold. Matt was a little hesitant about our plan, though. I had already showered and was dressing in front of the bathroom mirror before he got out of bed and wandered to the bathroom.

"You going to shower?" I asked, looking at the clock. It was already nine, and we had three different addresses to visit.

"Yeah," he mumbled, yawning, as he patted my butt on the way to the toilet. "I'll be quick, don't worry."

"I really want to get going," I said.

"Hey," he responded, with a serious look on his face. "If we don't find her, that's okay, too, right?"

I frowned. "We have three freaking addresses. Of course, we're going to find her."

"I don't know. I just don't want you to be upset if we don't."

"Matt."

"Isabell."

"Matthew. We're going to find her today, and I don't need your negativity. Get showered, get dressed, then we're going. I'm going to go get you some coffee."

I left him in the bathroom, but his words rang in my ears all the way downstairs to the breakfast area and all the way back. What if we didn't find her? What would I do? Although some part of me had considered the possibility of coming up empty, it wasn't a train of thought I'd pursued. In fact, I'd completely turned my back on it. I was determined to find her. We had information we weren't supposed to have, and if we visited these addresses and asked questions, surely we would be led to her whereabouts, and I'd be able to ask her all my questions. Right?

When I delivered his coffee to the bathroom sink, he called to me from inside the shower to come in, but I ignored him. I put my hair up in a ponytail and sat down on the bed to map out the location of each of the three addresses on the map as I listened to the gentle tumble of water in the shower. By the time we left the motel, it was already ten-thirty. I felt frantic that we were so behind in the plans I'd laid out for the day. Matt, however, seemed calm and thoughtful. His eyes were a clear sea-green, indicating his light mood.

"Did you mean it when you said that we might not find anything?" I probed him as we drove to the first address. I was looking for a fight. Though he'd previously been so good about supporting me through this, his comment this morning simultaneously worried and irked me. I was having trouble understanding why—after coming this far on the journey with me—he would suddenly begin preparing me for the possibility of coming up empty.

"I just want you to be prepared for whatever happens," he responded.

I didn't answer. My stomach was in knots as we drove; I thought about what I would say when we arrived.

Only minutes later, we pulled into the driveway of an old rundown house in a neighborhood that had likely seen better days. Grass and shrubs grew over cracked sidewalks, and the house that's driveway we sat in had chipped paint and foil inside the windows.

"Here we are," Matt said and put the truck into park. Nervously, I gathered up my journal and pen to take to the door.

"Do you want me to come with you?" he asked as I unbuckled my seatbelt.

"You can if you want."

He nodded. We walked up to the door together and knocked. There was no doorbell in sight. After a couple of minutes, we knocked again and, finally, an older man opened the wooden door and looked out at us through the screen.

"Hi," I said, doing my best to put on a brave face. "My name is Izzie, and I'm looking for a woman named Carole Wilson. I've got records that show she lived here at some point or maybe still does?"

"Carole Wilson?" he asked. "I'm real sorry, but I can't help you. I've rented this house for the past two years, but I

don't know much about who might have lived here before."
He moved back to close the door.

"Wait," I said. "Could you possibly give me your landlord's phone number? Maybe they might know something."

He stood still, looking at me hard. "Why are you looking for her? She in trouble or something?"

"Actually, she's my birthmother. I'm trying to find her."

He grunted and stood there staring at us for what seemed like an eternity. "Yeah, I guess I could give you my landlord's number." He turned and walked back into the house. Matt and I stood on the porch waiting in silence.

He came back and recited a name and number for me to write down. I thanked him, and he nodded before closing the door.

"So, first things first," I said to Matt as we climbed back into the truck. "Let's call the landlord and also the phone number we got from the agency. Those might be our best bets."

"I think that's a good idea," Matt said. "Let me just find a good place to park that isn't this man's driveway." He backed out into the street, driving until he found a commercial street. We parked at a Walmart, and I got out my phone from the glove compartment. I handed Matt's over, too.

There were two missed calls from my parents. Twinging with temporary guilt, I made a mental note to call them back. I had gone much farther than the lake this time, and though I'd informed them that I would be taking this trip, they hadn't asked for details—and I hadn't offered many up.

Sitting with my journal and a pen in my lap, I first called the number from the agency. The line immediately beeped a three-toned error and the message: "Sorry, the phone number you are trying to reach has been disconnected or is no longer in service."

I hung up and looked over at Matt. He shrugged. I dialed the landlord's number next.

The phone rang several times before redirecting to voice-mail. I took a deep breath as I listened to the recorded message and, after the beep, said, "Hello. My name is Isabell Quince, and I'm looking for one of your past tenants at 1484 Lionshead Road by the name of Carole Wilson. She is my birthmother, and I found records that said she lived there in the past. If you could, please call me back." I left my phone number and hung up.

Sighing, I pulled the map back out. "Next one?" My spirits were beginning to sink, but I still had hope.

Matt leaned over the console to kiss me, but I turned and gave him my cheek. My mouth was too dry from nerves for any kissing.

The next address led us to an apartment building across from a rundown shopping center full of shops with things like specialty tobacco, tattoos, and adult toys.

Upon seeing the shops, Matt nudged me and grinned. "Looks like we could get some shopping done after this stop. Want to get a tattoo? You're eighteen now."

I laughed. "Careful. I'm having a life crisis. I just might take you up on that."

He chuckled and pulled into the parking lot by the apartment's front office. Same as before, I took a deep breath, and we walked in together.

There wasn't anybody in sight. We stood at the reception and looked around.

"Anybody here?" Matt called after a couple of minutes. Before we knew it, a skinny young brunette came out of nowhere.

"Hey, there, can I help you?" she asked.

"Yes, actually. I'm looking for my birthmother. Her name is Carole Wilson, and I've got records showing that she lived here at some point. Could you help me out?"

"Oh, gosh," the brunette said. "You know, we're not supposed to give out that kind of information."

"Yeah," I said, hoping to sound as if I had expected this answer, although I hadn't at all. "I was just hoping that maybe you could help point me in the right direction. Anything helps." I put on my best puppy eyes.

"Oh." She looked at me with pity. "You know what? What the hell. Let me see what I can find for you. Come on back." She led us to an office. We both sat down in the chairs in front of her desk as she logged onto the computer.

"Carole—what was her name? Let me see if I can find her records in here."

"Wilson," I said. "Thank you so much for doing this. It means a lot."

She smiled at me and began typing. As she waited for the screen to load, she turned back my way. "Sorry, the computer is a little slow. It just melts my heart, you coming here. I've got a cousin who's adopted, but she came from overseas. She'd be jealous of you for having somewhere to start on the journey to finding your birthmother."

"I've got a couple of older cousins adopted from overseas, too. Seeing my aunt and uncle adopt kids really helped my parents through the process," I offered.

"That's great," she said. "It looks like Carole did live here for a while. About a year ago her lease came up, and she didn't renew. Had a couple of roommates. Doesn't look like she left a forwarding address, though."

I sighed. "Okay," I said, trying to grapple with a third dead-end in one morning.

"I'm so sorry, sweetie. I wish there was something I could do to help."

"What about the names of the roommates?" Matt asked. "Maybe we could look them up in the phone book?"

"That's an idea," the brunette said. I got out my journal and pen and, once ready, she listed the three names to me: Angela, Kat, and Liza. "I've actually got a phonebook up at the front desk. They delivered them a month or so ago."

We followed her back to the front and pored through the phonebook looking for names and addresses. Only one of the listed names included an address and number. I copied it down.

"Thank you so much for all your help," I said, handing the phonebook back to her.

"Don't you tell on me," she teased. "I'm glad I could help out. Good luck!" She waved us out the door, and I got back into the truck feeling lighter.

"Let me call this number real quick and see if anything turns up," I said. "Better we call before driving all the way over."

I dialed the number. After about three rings, a woman answered the phone.

"Hello?" she said.

"Hi," I said. "Is this Angela?"

"This is she."

"Hey, my name is Isabell Quince, and I'm looking for Carole Wilson. She's my birthmother. I found out that you lived in an apartment with her and was hoping you could help me find her."

"Oh," said the woman. "Oh, wow. Um." The line went quiet for a moment.

"Ma'am?" I prompted.

"Yeah," she said. "Sorry, it's just... It's a big shock, you calling me. I didn't know."

"I'm so sorry to call you out of the blue like this," I said, "but I'm actually in town looking for her. I got some past addresses from the adoption agency and thought it wouldn't hurt to come see what I could find."

"Sure, of course. You hungry?"

"What?"

"I just mean, if you're in town, do you want to have lunch? It's about that time, and I could tell you what I know," she said.

"Sure," I affirmed, looking over at Matt with an ecstatic expression. "I'd love that, thank you! Where can we meet?"

She gave me directions to a burger joint a couple of minutes away, and we agreed to meet her there in about fifteen minutes.

When I hung up the phone, Matt pointed excitedly at the map. "This must be her address. The address we copied down from the phonebook is also the last address we have on the list. And it's close to that restaurant. I think we're getting really close!"

I squealed. "Oh my God, oh my God, oh my God, I can't breathe. What if we *really* find her? Are these questions enough? What do you think? Did you think this was going to happen?" I held out my visibly shaking hands in front of me.

Matt laughed. "I really didn't. I didn't think we'd get this far." He reached over and gave my hand a squeeze. My heart felt like it might explode out of my chest.

On the way to the burger joint, I smoked another cigarette to calm my nerves. I couldn't wait to hear what Angela had to say about my actual real-life birthmother.

CHAPTER 8

MEETING THE PARTNERS IN CRIME

———

When we arrived at the burger joint, a short curvy woman with dark brown hair and thick makeup was waiting for us under the shaded overhang at the front. After trudging through the sun's intense heat waves of midday, I hesitantly asked, "Angela?" before reaching out to shake her hand. She glanced at Matt.

"Sorry, this is my boyfriend, Matt," I said. "He couldn't resist the idea of a road trip, so he came along to help me find Carole."

Matt smiled and shook her hand, then we went inside and ordered burgers at the counter. Once we sat down with our drinks, I asked her if it was okay if I took notes while she told us what she knew.

She nodded. "Sure. I can't imagine what it must be like looking for your birthmother. I didn't even know she had a child, to be honest. But I want to do right by you. You deserve to know some things about her."

I got out my journal and pen.

"I lived with Carole in a couple of different places," she started. "We were roommates for about two years. Both of us struggled with keeping a job, but between the two of us, we could usually manage to keep a roof over our heads, even if we were a little late on rent sometimes. We got into trouble a couple of times, too. I don't know if you'd want to visit the police station or if they'd even release some of the information to you, but we've both made some pretty bad decisions. It was only in this past year that I began to clean up my act and keep a steady job. The thing is, though, that even as I started getting clean and all, Carole hit some hard times."

"What kind of bad decisions?" I asked.

She winced and looked down at her lap before answering. "Drugs mostly, prostitution, petty theft."

I nodded, and she continued.

"I don't know how much you know about her, but she has paranoid schizophrenia. When she's got money for her meds, she's usually okay. But she doesn't always have the money. The last time I saw her, she didn't have the money or the desire to be on her meds."

"Wait," I said. "I did know about the schizophrenia, but all I know about it is that hallucinations happen, and it can be passed down genetically. Could you explain how it affected Carole?"

"Oh," said Angela. "Well, for Carole, she'd get really delusional about things and her anxiety would spiral, sometimes to the point that she wouldn't be able to function. Sometimes she saw things, but mostly she heard things. She would sometimes have weird little episodes where she'd get confused and not be able to explain how she felt. I never really understood much of what went on in her head, but we worked street corners together, and it just made sense that we look out for each other." She winced as she said this. I knew it must have embarrassed her to tell an eighteen-year-old about the things she'd regretted doing, so I did my best to look supportive and understanding.

"As you can imagine, our friendship was pretty rocky at times," she sighed. "But now it's definitely over."

"What? Why is it over?" I asked.

"She had this nasty boyfriend. He's schizophrenic, too, and has much worse on his jail record than we do. I don't know. They connected in this weird way, and about six months ago, she walked out to live with him."

"So, she's living with her boyfriend now?" I asked. "Where are they?"

"Well, that's the thing." She shifted uncomfortably in her seat. Just then, a waitress delivered our burgers to the table. We paused to eat, and I took the time to scribble more notes as I waited patiently for Angela to continue.

"Her boyfriend," Angela said as she opened ketchup packets for her fries, "didn't exactly have a place to live. He stayed with us for a while, but it didn't last. When he left, so did she. They left to go live out on the streets."

I took a bite of my burger and raised my eyebrows. This story was happening too fast for me to write down properly. Hopefully, I'd be able to understand my notes later.

Angela paused to eat, so I picked up the conversation.

"So, she's homeless now, and you're done being her friend because her boyfriend is such a jerk," I summarized, trying to make sure I had it all right.

"Well, yeah, but that's not the whole story. Her boyfriend, Rick, actually got picked up again, and last I heard, he's sitting in jail."

"So, where is she?"

She shrugged. "I don't know. Nobody I know who knows her has seen her since he got picked up. She's just gone."

"Gone? Where could she have gone?"

"You would think she'd still be wandering around homeless," she said. "But she's just disappeared."

We sat and ate in silence for a few minutes. I turned over this information in my head. Finally, I decided to ask what the boyfriend's full name was. She gave it to me, and I wrote it down. Maybe I could look him up in jail, pay him a visit.

"Is there... anything else you can tell me about her?" I asked. "I just want to know more about what she was like, who she was as a person, you know?"

"Um, sure," she said, looking up at the ceiling to think. "On her good days, she was wildly creative. She liked to write short stories and poems." She paused. "She also had a sister who checked in on her every once in a while. Her dad would, too, but they didn't really get along that well. She was charming as hell when she wanted to be. And she could hold her own in a fight." Angela paused again to wipe her mouth with a napkin.

"I don't know that much about her, to tell the truth. It was only two years that we were together, and the last one was a complete nightmare. I don't know much about her life before I met her. I'm sorry. I wish I could tell you more."

I nodded. "It's okay. This is really helpful." I took a minute to scribble down some last notes before closing my journal to focus solely on eating. We finished our lunch with small talk. Matt held most of the conversation; I had fallen into my head.

As we came to the end of our burgers, I asked one last question.

"What do you know about her boyfriend, Rick? Do you think he'd have much to tell me if we went and found him in jail?"

"He's a pretentious asshole," she said abruptly. "He's violent and hateful and convinced that he's met some twisted version of God. I don't know what would happen if you visited him. I honestly don't think you should. All I know is that he's a despicable human. If you do visit him, just know that he's a bona fide lunatic."

I nodded solemnly. Matt reached for my hand under the table and squeezed. We left the restaurant in a new kind of mood, one I didn't know how to express. The sun had fallen behind a pile of large, gray clouds, and the thick heat, even under clouded cover, sat on our shoulders as we walked out. We both thanked Angela for having lunch and telling us so much about Carole, then got in the truck and watched as she drove off.

"You okay?" Matt asked.

"I don't know," I said. I really didn't. I'd come to this lunch thinking that I'd finally found a path to my birthmother. But after listening to Angela explain such heavy histories, brief though they were, I felt completely lost. Mental illness, jail time, disappearances, and a terrible boyfriend. Maybe it would be better if I didn't find her at all.

"You want to head back home?" he asked quietly.

"No," I said, making up my mind on the spot. "I want to go to the jail."

"Are you sure?"

"Yeah," I said. "But first I want to sit here and clean up my notes and try to sort through what Angela told us. It was a lot. I don't really know what to think of it."

"Okay," he said. "Do you mind if I call my mom while you write?"

"Go ahead," I said. "Tell her hello for me. I need to call my parents, too."

"Might be better if I call them," he said. "They won't be as upset if it's me calling.

"Yeah. Probably."

I opened my journal to the page with notes from our lunch conversation and put my finger as a bookmark before opening it to a clean page. I went back and forth between the notes, carefully writing a cleaner and more detailed copy on the fresh sheet of paper. I strained my memory for as many actual quotes as I could decipher from my sloppily written notes.

Meanwhile, Matt called his mom and explained that we were in Albuquerque looking for my birthmother. After hanging up with his mom, he proceeded to call mine.

My mom let out an audible breath of relief when she answered the phone and heard his voice. She immediately asked if we were okay. He told her the whole story and apologized for not calling sooner. He gently reminded her how important this journey was to me, told her we were being careful, and that we'd be home in a day or two.

By the time he was done with parental phone calls, I'd cleaned up my notes and was ready to embark on the last visit of the day. After finding the local jail on the map, we drove in silence. I didn't know what was going through Matt's head, but I was absolutely petrified. I wasn't sure about this at all, yet knew I'd regret not visiting the boyfriend in jail if we didn't go.

On the drive over, my phone rang, and I picked it up. It was the landlord from the first address returning my call.

"Thanks for calling back," I said, then asked if he had any information about his previous tenant.

"Not much," he admitted. "Carole lived there for about a year, paid about half of her rent on time, and didn't take very good care of the place. She didn't leave a forwarding address when she left, either, so I can't help you there. I'm very sorry."

"That's okay," I said and thanked him for returning my call before hanging up.

Matt reached over and gave my thigh a gentle squeeze. Soon we pulled up to the local jail.

* * *

"Ready?" he asked while parking in front of the jail—a flat gray building with a paint job that looked as battered as I felt.

"As I'll ever be," I responded.

I explained to the young policeman sitting behind the counter who I wanted to visit and why. "I'm looking for my birthmother, and I spoke with one of her old roommates who said that her boyfriend, Rick, might be able to help me find where she is. According to her roommate, he's the last person who's seen her."

The policeman nodded and asked us both for our IDs. We took them out and handed them over. He made copies, then made us sign in as visitors with the time and date.

"Visiting hours end at five," he said and nodded toward the clock. It was a little after three. "Please have a seat, and I'll let you know if you'll be able to visit with Rick in a moment." He disappeared into the back. We sat on the cold plastic chairs in the lobby to wait. I looked uneasily around at the walls, filled with cheap frames holding announcements, rules, and information. Matt put his hand on my knee.

When the policeman finally returned, he opened the door for us to follow him back. We were led to a row of booths with windows and phones, just like in the movies. A couple of other people were there, too, and suddenly, I realized that

I had no idea what Rick looked like. Luckily, the policeman leading us in took us straight to him.

On the other side of the glass was a man with cloudy blue eyes and shaggy brown hair peppered with gray. His suntanned skin was noticeably weathered. There was only one phone and chair, so I sat down. Matt stood behind me, a hand on my shoulder. I picked up the phone.

I wasn't sure what the policeman had told him, so I gave him the whole story. "My name is Isabell, and I was adopted eighteen years ago. I'm looking for my birthmother, Carole Wilson, and one of her old roommates, Angela, told me I could find you here. She said you were the last person she knew Carole was with."

"Yeah, the officer told me," he said flatly.

"Do you know where Carole is?"

"Not the slightest, honey," he said and laughed.

"Well," I said, slightly alarmed at this. "What can you tell me about her? Weren't you dating her at some point before you ended up here?"

He laughed some more. I waited for him to stop. My hands began to shake.

"I can't believe you're sitting right here in front of me," he said, still laughing. "I didn't know she had a kid. God, this is crazy. They say I'm crazy and then something like this happens." He shook his head violently before refocusing on me.

"She didn't tell you she had a kid?"

"Couldn't believe a word that came out of that woman's devil mouth," he smirked. "But I should have known, the way she wrote all those letters to a girl named Rose."

"What kind of things did she write in those letters?"

"Oh, all of our secrets. I had to burn them all." He laughed again, then abruptly pulled his face into a snarl. "I did it for her own good, though."

My eyes widened in shock. I wasn't sure how to respond to him, and upon seeing my reaction, he laughed some more. I moved uneasily in my seat and waited for him to stop.

"Why did you have to burn them? What secrets?" I asked. The phone was shaking noticeably in my hand.

"You wouldn't understand," he said. "You aren't one of us, I can tell. You don't have the Sight like we do. Carole and I, that's why we were together. We can see things, know things that other people can't see, can't know. The doctors want to give us medicine, but really, they don't want people like us knowing what we do. Too much power, you know." He looked at me sternly.

"Okay," I said. "So, you were together before you got thrown in jail?"

"Yep," he said.

"What happened?"

"What happened is that I got thrown in jail."

"Why?"

He let out a loud and sudden guffaw; I instinctively recoiled. Matt's grip on my shoulder tightened.

"They said one of the girlies I picked up off the street was underage," he leered. "The truth is, she just couldn't handle me and went running to tattle. She didn't have any of them bruises or cuts when she ran out on me, but the pictures after, she cut herself up real bad."

I stayed silent.

"You can believe what you want about me," he said. "But me and your mom, now, that was a real good time until it ended."

"Where is she now?" I asked again.

"Oh, she's gone," he laughed. "I told her to run, and she did. She ran and ran."

"Where did you tell her to run to?"

He leaned close to the glass before answering me. "I told her to run 'til she couldn't run anymore. The cops in this town, they're cracking down on all of us who don't want to live in little houses with street numbers and telephones. They don't want us wandering the world and exposing the truth."

"So, you don't know where she is?"

"Gone," he laughed. "She's gone."

I stared him down for as long as I could before I felt the heat of suppressed tears bubbling up.

"Is there anything else you can tell me about her?" I asked.

"Nope." He smiled, and without waiting for more, I hung up the phone. He sat there with the phone to his ear even after I'd gotten up. I followed Matt and the police officer out to the front lobby again. I thanked the officer, and we walked out the door.

When we were back in the truck and Matt had turned on the air conditioning, I sighed. He reached over to hold my hand.

"Izzie," he began. "I know today wasn't what you wanted it to be, but after learning what we have, I think you're truly better off this way."

"Yeah," I said quietly. "I guess so."

He squeezed my hand. "Now what?"

"It's almost four," I said. "I don't really want to drive home today."

"So, let's find a place to crash, and we'll drive home tomorrow. How's that sound?"

"That sounds good," I said.

"Do you want to pick a place from the map, or should we just drive around for a bit?"

"Let's drive around."

So, he turned up the music, I lit a cigarette, and we drove.

CHAPTER 9

THE AFTERMATH

———

We spent a long evening at the motel. Matt passed the time by watching TV, clicking through channels now and then. Every so often, he'd lean over and kiss me, but I wasn't interested in his feeble attempts to cheer me up. I moved away from him on the bed so I could flip through the pages of my notebook.

The book wasn't going to work. The whole outline was trash. The idea of a three-part narrative made me sick to my stomach. I didn't feel better at all for what we had found; in fact, I felt worse. And despite having learned so much, I felt emptier than I ever had before. Though I wished I could purge all the anger and sadness and loss by burying my head in a pillow and crying, I felt more like a deep abandoned well—dried up and hollow.

I wrote down what I could about my interactions with everybody on the trip so far: the adoption agency, the old man in the old house, the apartment manager, the previous roommate, and the boyfriend in jail. Writing all of it took the rest of the evening. It was the only way I knew how to separate myself from the instant depression I'd fallen into. But even writing everything down added to the numbing sensation that was quickly beginning to overwhelm me.

Matt ordered pizza once he realized I wasn't going to be dragged out to dinner after the day I'd had. I didn't eat. The smell of pepperoni just about made me gag. By the time the room began to lose natural light from the window, as evening turned to night, I was so exhausted I could hardly think straight.

Matt, for his part, eventually turned off the TV and convinced me to go to sleep. But after we'd brushed our teeth and turned the lights off, my mind was still restless. After trying and failing to cheer me up with kisses and attempting to give a back massage I was too tense to enjoy, he rolled over and fell asleep. I lay awake until about two in the morning, tossing and turning, unable to put my mind to rest. I finally fell asleep out of pure exhaustion.

The next morning, we quietly packed up and set out for the journey home. About thirty minutes into the car ride home, Matt tried again to cheer me up, this time by telling me about a ridiculous dream he'd had the night before.

"Want to play?" he asked me in a teasing voice. "There were dinosaurs involved, and a disco ball."

I managed a laugh. "Yeah, I've had some pretty weird dreams on this trip, too." But as I began to think about all the strange things that had populated my subconscious lately, an idea hit me like lightning.

"Hold on," I said, reaching down to open my backpack. I pulled out both journals and a pen.

"Forget that three-part narrative. I won't get anything else out of my parents, you were right, and we didn't find my birthmother, so it just won't work, but…" I trailed off and opened the new journal to the first gloriously empty page, then flipped through the one that held all of my adventures and notes from the trip.

"But what?" he asked.

"But I know what story I *can* write."

"Yours?"

"No, no. The dreams! Just let me write."

Without another word, I began writing furiously and didn't stop until we hit the city limit sign of our hometown.

* * *

The drive home from Albuquerque had been our shortest yet. The afternoon was young.

"Can you just drop me off at my house?" I asked. "My parents probably want to see me home for a few days."

"Sure," he said. "Want to get lunch or something tomorrow?"

"Yeah." I smiled. "That sounds good."

He kissed me goodbye after pulling into the driveway. I gathered all my things and walked in the front door.

My mom was sitting in the living room and cried out upon seeing me. "Izzie! We've been worried sick! Why didn't you call? You're home!" She rushed to hug me.

"Sorry, Mama," I said sheepishly. "I didn't mean for the trip to be so long, but I just had to go find things out for myself."

To my surprise, she nodded and wiped a tear out of her eye. "I'm just glad you made it home."

I patted her awkwardly on the back. When she let go, she looked me up and down then said in a strange, tentative voice, "Did you… find what you were looking for?"

I looked at her unbrushed hair, proof that she had been sleeping on the couch the entire time I'd been gone—the same way she did when I stayed out past curfew or she knew I'd snuck out. I didn't know how to respond.

"I don't know. We didn't find her, but I think maybe that's for the best?"

She nodded sagely. I was too tired to tell or care if she was holding back from telling me *I told you so* but, to my surprise, she quickly pivoted to the warm mom I knew as a five-year-old.

"Put your things down, I'll do your laundry. You need to get some rest. You look exhausted," she said.

I dropped my duffle bag and pillow on the floor but kept my backpack on. "I think I'm going to go lay down. Wake me up for dinner?"

"Sure," she said while shooing me to my room.

Though I'd planned to continue my writing spree once I'd closed the door, the minute I sat on my bed, the only clean spot in my entire room, exhaustion overwhelmed me. I crawled under the covers and slept until dinner.

Though both of my parents were happy to see me home, they didn't ask many questions over dinner and, somehow, they both looked as if they'd aged while I was gone. I wasn't sure how to react to this silence or to the sudden realization that I had exhausted them with all I'd put them through. After all, I'd disappeared after graduation to drink, left on a three-day road trip with my boyfriend, and stayed in hotels while only calling once. Where were the lectures? Where was the disapproval? It was Ronnie who finally piped up and asked where I'd been.

I gave her the short answer. I told her I went to the adoption agency to find out more about my birthmother, then ended up in New Mexico trying to hunt her down. I mentioned a few things about the people I'd met but left out the things I thought were too much: the boyfriend in jail, the ex-roommate's lifestyle. I concluded by saying that Carole was gone. I didn't repeat the sentiment I'd shared with our mom earlier that maybe this conclusion was for the best. I suddenly didn't feel so sure about it.

Ronnie watched me carefully as I explained, then after I was done, asked, "Are you glad you went? Even if you didn't find her?"

"Actually, yeah. I'm really glad I went."

She nodded and smiled at me. We ate the rest of our dinner in silence.

As I helped transport dirty dishes to the sink afterward, my dad caught me and asked if I'd done any more thinking on what to do in the fall. He was hoping I would go to school, but I told him I wasn't sure yet. He nodded and encouraged me to spend some time thinking about it.

"It'll be here before you know it," he said.

But when I returned to my room after dinner, I didn't think about what was coming next at all. How could I? I could barely map out how I felt in that moment. I had a lot of writing to do. So, I stayed up all night penning the beginnings of a book I'd begun that very morning. When I finally fell asleep, face down on my journal and pen in hand, the sun was beginning to peek through my windows.

* * *

Lunch the next day with Matt proved to be an unexpectedly awkward return to the real world, in which I had just graduated high school and everybody, including him, wanted to know what I'd be doing next. It was also apparently the world in which Matt had forgotten how to act like a normal person. He kept smiling nervously at me and picking at his food.

"Are you okay?" I asked.

"I've been thinking," Matt began, and I looked into his green eyes. "I'm going back to school in the fall, and I've been wondering what you're going to do."

I didn't say anything. It didn't seem like he was done with his thought, despite the expectant look on his face.

"I know that you probably feel a little upside down after turning eighteen and going through all of this. I mean, we only got home yesterday, so I don't really expect you to know exactly what you're doing in the fall, but…"

"My dad asked me the same question last night."

"Well," he said, "it's probably about time you start thinking about it. I know I've already said this, but I'd love for you to come stay with me, whether you sign up for classes or decide to take a gap year. I just want to know where your head's at."

I furrowed my brow. Though I hadn't put serious thought into answering this question, it wasn't an unexpected one. I couldn't figure out why Matt seemed so apprehensive asking about it.

"I get it if you don't know yet, but promise you'll tell me when you do?"

"I promise," I said and reached over to link my pinky in his. "But I don't know how I feel about living together, especially after we've been apart for so long."

He frowned.

"Right now," I continued, "my head is in this book that I started writing yesterday. I think this is what I need to focus on right now."

He nodded, but his face remained serious.

"Past that, I have no idea what's going to happen or where I'll be going," I said.

"That's okay," he replied. "But if it counts for anything, I really think that, school or not, you should come stay with me next year. I won't be staying in the dorms anymore. I've got a job lined up with one of my buddies. I'm going to get a little one-bedroom apartment, and I think it would be good for both of us."

"I don't know," I said. "I just haven't had the time to give it much thought. I mean, this past year has been pretty hard on us being apart for so long. But then again, don't you think it's done us some good, too?"

His cheeks went a little pink at this. "I mean, I don't know. I've missed you. And I still miss you. I don't know how to say it." He paused. "It's different now."

"What's different?" I didn't know how to take this. "Why are you blushing?"

"I'm not blushing," he argued, cheeks getting pinker by the second. "I just mean, you've changed, our relationship has changed, and I want to know where it's going. That's all."

"Are you trying to figure out where I'm going so you can figure out whether to break up with me or not?"

"What? No," he shot back, flustered. "I just—I know it's selfish, but it's been all about you ever since April, and at some point, I want you to figure out where you're going because, yeah, I want to know what I'm supposed to be preparing for. Are we going to say goodbye again at the end of the summer? Are you coming with me? I just want to know, is all." By this point, his cheeks were fully red, his eyes neon green with annoyance.

"Well, Matt," I said, my voice rising in irritation, "I don't know how I've changed. I'm sorry I've been distant, I'm sorry I've been so hyper-focused on trying to figure out who the hell I'm supposed to be now that all this information about my birthmother has been dumped on me. I don't know where I'm going. And I don't know when I'll know."

"I get it. It's been a hell of a time, but I've been trying to help you. Is it worth nothing that I took you on this road trip to help you find answers? I just want to know what comes next," he responded, angry. "It's not that hard, Izzie."

I got up from the table abruptly at this. "I'll call you when I know. How about that?" I walked out to my car, not caring to look behind me as I left.

When I got home, I put my phone in my underwear drawer and sat down to write. Whatever was happening with Matt would blow over. It always did. But at that moment, I needed to focus on the story I was writing. Until I finished it, I didn't think I'd feel like a whole human being. So, I wrote and wrote and wrote.

I didn't look up for a month and a half. And this is what I wrote:

PART 2

ROSE'S LOCKET

CHAPTER 10

THE FIRST MYSTERIOUS BEGINNING

———

One spring night, under a waxing moon and with a slight wind, the residents of the village of Zophren slept soundly in their feather beds, completely unaware of hooves quietly trotting into town from the southeast.

Nobody woke up to the gentle whoosh of disturbed water making waves. Nobody was aware at all that Isabell's great-great-great-great-great-grandmother had arrived. Or at least, that's how the legend goes.

It wasn't until dawn—when the doves cooed, the roosters crowed, and the baby on the island in the middle of the lake cried—that anyone stirred in their beds.

William's wife, Marie, was the first to run out onto the dirt path next to the shore in her nightgown to locate the strange sound. A strong wail echoed against the sides of the mountains north of the village and crashed back. By some divine twist of fate, William, the town historian, would soon be putting his own name in the history books, but he didn't know that at the time. All he knew was that his wife wanted him to put on pants and row his wooden boat to the island that sat in the middle of the lake, which sat in the middle of the village.

By the time he pushed off, the rest of the residents had heard the commotion and gathered on the dirt path along the shoreline.

The men hollered from the shore.

"Do you need anything?"

"Should we bring our boats, too?"

"Why's a baby on the island?"

"Town meeting this morning!"

The children splashed in the shallow waters, and the women stood nearby whispering in huddles.

"Is it a miracle?"

"But nobody's been pregnant."

"How did a baby get on the island?"

"Who will care for it?"

The roosters kept crowing as the sun lifted above the horizon, and the doves kept cooing while William rowed out.

When he reached the island, he found the tiny baby cradled in a wicker basket hanging from a tree branch. He peered into the basket and the baby, surprised to see him, stopped crying. Little heaves of exhaustion from crying so hard shook the infant's entire frame. He carefully reached in and pulled the baby, wrapped in white linen, into his arms. William noticed that tucked just under the linen, a gold chain with a golden heart-shaped locket was draped around the infant's neck.

They looked each other over, and William rewrapped the linen blanket around the baby's feet. He carried it to the boat, leaving the basket to hang in the tree. Holding it tightly against his chest, he tried to warm the small body with his own. Something about the complete improbability of finding a baby on the island spoke to him; it was out of the strangeness of the situation that he felt a practical solution begin to fall into place.

William slowly rowed back to shore with the newborn, who had small tufts of brown hair and big blue eyes.

The whole town crowded around the boat to see the wonder and Paige, the town's babysitter, produced a bottle of milk.

William held the strange new baby as it gulped down the milk and regarded him. Only slightly aware of his wife's guiding hand on his arm and the chatter of townspeople around him, he followed Marie back into the house and sat down, awestruck.

Marie bustled about the house, getting dressed and making breakfast while William silently contemplated the fate of the small infant in his arms.

"Let me hold the baby while you get dressed, William," she said, handing him a bowl of oatmeal. Her heart bumped violently in her chest at the sight of his eyes focused on the baby.

William glanced up. "Oh, I don't need to go in today."

"William," Marie said sternly. "There's a town meeting in thirty minutes about your new friend. Now go get dressed."

Reluctantly, he handed the baby over then set about eating his oatmeal and readying to go into town. When he returned from dressing, Marie had already washed the baby in the tub and wrapped her in fresh linens. A girl. After seeing the engraving of a single rose on the front of the baby's locket, she had plucked a rose from her garden outside and pinned it to the linen on the baby's chest. William smiled at the flower, reaching out for Marie to hand her back over.

They retired to their front porch—as was the custom when the town was gathering for an impromptu meeting—and waited for their neighbors to the east to begin the procession west and around the lake to the town hall. William and Marie gazed out across the water, both lost in thought wondering the same thing in different words.

After a moment, William looked at Marie. "What do you think is going to happen?"

"I… well, I don't know. This is so unexpected," Marie said, looking back at him. "What do you want to happen?"

"I think we should raise her. We've been thinking of having children, haven't we?" he asked, scanning her eyes, searching deep.

She met his eyes, then turned back to look out at the lake. "I think so, too," she answered, swallowing hard the elation at this possibility. They'd been childless for years, and now she might be a mother. The lake was beginning to reflect the soft pink and orange tones of the sunrise.

She smiled at him and reached for the baby, pulling her to her chest. She let free a deep sigh of relief at the thought that she had a good chance of loving a baby all her own. William's heart soared at the sight of them.

When the neighbors walked up the path and stood in front of their porch, the two looked up. The procession had arrived. The group chanted:

"It's time to speak our words.
It's time to hear the news.
Gather, people, gather.
It's time to vote and choose.

Citizens of Zophren,
Down to City Hall!
Citizens of Zophren,
Come one, come all!"

William and Marie stood once the chant was over and walked down the steps to join the procession. The neighbors' eyes followed the baby with curiosity, but they waited until everyone began walking to ask their questions.

"What's going to happen?"

"Was there a note?"

"Are you going to keep it?"

"Is it a boy or a girl?"

William grinned at all the questions, giddy with the idea that he'd soon be asking the town for permission to keep the infant and raise her.

"It's a girl. I think Marie and I want to keep her," he said, and Marie smiled as everybody looked to the baby in her arms with loving eyes and nods of approval.

"Of course! Who'd be better?"

"You've got my vote!"

"You'll make wonderful parents!"

Soon, the procession arrived at the next door. They dutifully recited their chant and gathered another couple from their porch.

"What's the news?" the woman next door asked, joining the procession.

"They're going to keep her," someone replied from somewhere near the front. Happy chatter followed.

"Ooh, any thoughts on names?" she asked, linking her arm in Marie's.

The whole group turned toward Marie as they walked, and she laughed in surprise.

"Oh, she had a little locket around her neck with a rose on it," she offered.

They paused to gather another family from their porch, chanting, then continued on their way discussing the blessings and challenges that came with parenthood. The remaining villagers were collected and, house by house, they decided that the best thing for the baby was to let William and Marie raise her.

By the time they got to City Hall, everybody sat down in their pews and wrote on their voting cards, *Baby should be raised by William and Marie.* By then, the name Rose had already been decided on. William and Marie stood up at the front of the hall and, together as per the town's custom for the official naming of a new baby, cried:

"Her name is Rose!
Now ours to raise,
We'll love her 'til the end of days!

Her name is Rose!
Now shout it loud!
Her name is Rose! We'll make her proud!"

Nobody bothered to read any other announcements. The chant "Rose! Rose! Rose!" rang through the streets as the villagers poured out of City Hall. The town spent the rest of the day celebrating by making food for the new parents, singing and dancing on the shore by the lake, and handmaking quilts, linens, and rattles for the newest member of Zophren.

As the afternoon grew into evening, they all sat together in the sunshine, basking in the warmth and excitement of new life.

And so, Rose's story began.

CHAPTER 11

MELODY

———

Rose grew into a happy, curious, and energetic child. At three years old, she was a rosy-cheeked toddler whose smile and subsequent dimples never went away. It was at this time that the next improbable story unfolded in the quiet village of Zophren.

Once old enough to follow her parents into town, she told her mom one day as they walked to the community garden, "I want a baby sister."

A dreamy smile came over Rose's face as she imagined someone to play with.

Marie smiled faintly. "Oh, is that so?"

The town's garden grew on the east side of the lake in long rows. Every day, people from the village came to help water, weed, and collect the food in baskets early in the morning or late in the evening. Rose's family preferred the evening. They would stroll alongside the lake before dinner with empty baskets to do their part each night.

"Hey, Marie!" Their next-door neighbor waved from across the rows. "Tomatoes are perfect today."

Marie and Rose came to stand next to her as she picked tomatoes. Rose began reaching for the ripe red fruits at the bottom of the stalks but couldn't quite detach them on her own. Marie bent down to help, then said, "Rose, baby, why don't you go dig up some potatoes?"

Rose nodded, then puckered her lips for a kiss. Marie kissed her and patted her head before Rose darted off to dig.

"I have some big news," Marie said to her neighbor, Beverly, a small blond-haired woman. Marie gave her friend a sly little smile.

"Oh, gossip hour, is it?" Beverly smiled. "Is it about Andy and Susan? I've heard that they have been bickering. You think I'd know being their neighbor, but if they do fight, it's not loud enough for us to hear."

"No, silly. I saw Susan earlier today at the post office, actually, and she told me she's sent off for some new books for the library."

"Well, what is it then? Out with it!"

Marie looked at Beverly and took a deep breath. She reached for her belly, still flat under her apron. "I'm pregnant."

Beverly's jaw dropped. "Oh, Marie! Oh!"

Marie smiled wide, and Beverly hugged her, laughing.

"How long have you known? Are you sure?"

"I'm sure. It's been two months now."

"I can't believe it. You spent so much time trying before Rose, but—" Beverly paused. "Does William know yet? Have you told anybody?"

"You're the first to know. I think I'm going to tell him tonight. I wanted to wait and make sure I didn't lose it, you know."

"How are you going to tell him? Fancy dinner? A stroll by the lake?"

"Well, I'm going to take Rose down to Henry's fish stand and get a good fish. I'll make a nice dinner and tell William then. I think he'll be happy. He was so happy when Rose came to us, you know."

"I know. It was sweet to see."

"It *was* sweet."

They both bent down to find the perfect purple onion, and when Marie looked over at Beverly, the sheer joy still hadn't left her friend's face. Marie smiled to herself. It felt more real now that she'd spoken the truth aloud. Her belly tightened as she stood up and arranged her produce in her wicker basket.

"You'll help me when the baby comes?" Marie asked.

"Of course, I will. When are you going to make the announcement to the town? You know you have to tell everybody formally. Otherwise, word will get around before you can."

"I think we'll do it tomorrow after the children are home from seeing Paige. I'm sure William will be so excited he won't be able to contain himself any longer than a day."

Beverly nodded, and Rose came wobbling across the garden with an armful of potatoes and a fistful of smashed blueberries. Her mouth and chin dripped with purple juice.

"Looks like we're ready to head home," Marie said to Beverly who shooed them away. Rose dumped her finds into the basket haphazardly, and they set off on their way.

Rose held her mom's hand and talked the whole way about the little creatures she had found in the garden: worms, ladybugs, rolly bugs, and a butterfly that looked like it had big eyes with eyelashes on its wings. Marie only half heard her, though; her mind was on William and what his reaction would be to the phenomenon happening deep within her.

When they reached Henry's stand on the dock by the lake, Rose ran off to find clam shells on the shore.

"Hi, Henry," Marie said. "I need a big fish. What do you have?"

"Oh, Marie, you're in luck," Henry said, reaching under the counter. "I caught the most beautiful trout today." He pulled out a long fish, scales sparkling in the sunlight.

"It's perfect," she said. "I'll take it."

Marie hid her secret under her green skirt as she walked into the house, a basket full of other ingredients for dinner still on her arm. William greeted them from his chair. Books and papers littered the table in front of him from studying all day. Marie was nervous about her announcement, and Rose hopped into his lap to tell him all about her day.

Marie kissed him on the head and left Rose in his lap, then went to the kitchen to prepare the celebratory dinner. She sang to herself one of the songs she'd learned in school as a child:

> "Far beyond, our world so small,
> There's a point where there is all-knowing.
> Who's to say what joys do fall?
> Who's to say where it is we're going?
>
> So live your days
> And enjoy it all.
> Drink the sun's rays,
> And greet the rainfall.
>
> Who's to say
> That it won't all go?
> Be here today and
> Great joy you'll know."

With the beat in her hips, she wiggled her toes across the wooden floor while she chopped, cut, seasoned, boiled, and baked. As she cleaned up and put the food in bowls, Rose wandered in to play at her feet, hoping for a bite before dinner.

She scooped up Rose and called for William. Once they were at the table, she brought over the plates and set them down, beaming.

"I have some news," she announced, still standing.

William chuckled and set his hands in his lap to wait politely for her to speak.

Marie paused for dramatic effect, then said, "I'm going to have a baby."

William's smile froze, time wobbled for him; the words echoed lazily in the caverns of his skull, but they weren't quite words yet. All he heard was an enchanting pattern of sounds.

His body moved before his mind did, and he stood up to hug Marie, giving her a big kiss.

"What?" Rose shouted. "What? I'm baby!"

And they laughed, both swooping down to kiss her cheeks.

The thrill he felt about this child was different than what he had felt on the day Rose had come home. Rubbing his wife's flat belly, he marveled at the chance he had to be witness to the spectacular miracle of fatherhood—this time seeing it from the very start.

The next day, the minute Rose came home from school, they rang the bell on their front porch to alert the town of an announcement to be made. Their neighbors dutifully began the traditional procession down to City Hall. The sun shone brightly and the dirt on the path crunched under their feet as the townspeople fell into their traditional procession. But this time, nobody asked questions of William or Marie. As they walked, William held Marie's hand and gave her loving little squeezes as if to say, "Just wait 'til everybody hears the good news!"

After they'd stood in front of the town and proclaimed they were with child, everybody cheered and congratulated William and Marie on their way out the door. Though it wasn't the kind of all-day celebration that the arrival of Rose had called for, the joyous couple were excited to go home and begin clearing out space for their new arrival.

Finally, one chilly February night the next year, Rose sang her dad to sleep in the living room; they were impatiently waiting for the baby to come. Marie lay in bed, quietly enduring waves of pain as Beverly explained to her what would happen in a calming voice. As the waves grew stronger and Marie's body began to push the baby out, Rose began singing once more, her tiny voice lilting through the house to welcome her new baby sister.

> *"Sing a little melody*
> *Of happy, happy days.*
> *Sing a little melody*
> *Of starting brand new days.*
>
> *Daddy won't you sing with me?*
> *Mama won't you sing with me?*
> *Sing a little melody..."*

Rose's little sister, Melody, entered a world full of song. And when William awoke to the sound of one daughter singing and the other crying for the first time, tears of joy filled his eyes. He scooped Rose up and hurried to the bedroom. Marie was too exhausted to do anything but smile through her own tears as her family crowded around her and the new baby girl in her arms.

* * *

The years began to fly by, as they do when children are around. Rose grew into a slender and bright-eyed girl who continued to charm the town with her curiosity and wonder at the world, while Melody became her inseparable shadow. William and Marie were kept busy raising the two girls, and the town was delighted to help raise Melody as much as they were Rose.

Of course, as it often happens, Rose was the inspiration to many couples in the town to expand their families, and Melody was born right smack in the middle of a smattering of children.

It didn't surprise anyone after a few years to see Rose and Melody marching down the street with a line of children following them on a mission to do whatever was on their minds that particular day. Sometimes they would help out around town gardening or organizing the books in the library, but other times, they would swim in the lake, wander up the mountain, or play games in the dirt.

Their teacher and the town babysitter made sure to allow their studies to follow their curiosities so, as the years passed, apprentices soon filled the town's shops—one child loved making shoes, another recycling goods, another cleaning the water, and so on and so forth. Several of the children from this cohort began their own trades as couriers, inventors, or builders. This went on for many years, and by the time they were all teenagers, the town of Zophren had grown.

Rose became interested in her dad's job, in compiling and organizing the town's collection of literature. Though he worked specifically with historical records—which he liked to elaborate upon on a whim—she enjoyed helping construct the town's storybook. This book recorded, in narrative style, the town's goings-on as they happened. Despite how often her dad retold the story of finding her on the island with the locket around her neck, she would sometimes page through the town's record of the event afterward; it made her feel like she really did belong. She would sometimes peek at the pages from before she had arrived to see if there were any clues as to where she could have come from, but she never found anything of significance.

Marie, unlike William, preferred logical and sensible realms of thought, and Melody shared these sentiments. Marie often got onto William and Rose both for spending their days with too many books and asking too many "what-if" questions. Though happy to be the mother of two beautiful daughters, Marie hadn't recovered from childbirth very well. She was often tired and unable to do as much as she used to, especially in the way of cooking and sharing her recipes with the town. Melody took care of her on these dreary days, and they would share their thoughts.

Of course, when Melody wasn't busy taking care of her mom, she was following Rose around. Though she wasn't nearly as adventurous as her older sister, she was in awe of the way she commanded attention. While Rose seemed to have a clear path set for her through her interests and talents, Melody was unsure of what she could contribute. Comparison to her sister was one of her tragic flaws, and she knew it.

By the time Rose was seventeen, she had finished her schooling, become a full-time librarian, and was determined to put her own mark on the Zophren library. Melody, however, figured out that full-time work wasn't technically required in a town where everybody collaborated, so she found a boyfriend when she was fourteen—Silverton.

Silverton was the kind of boy Melody could show off at town events and take home to meet her parents, but the two of them often disappeared together for lengths of time. After these times, Melody would come home either elated or crying. She was good enough to hide her tears most of the time, but Rose would hear her creep into the house late at night; she knew that something was off about Silverton and the hold he had on her little sister.

Rose once confronted her sister about it, asking if everything was okay and if Melody's boyfriend was, in fact, treating her as he should.

Melody nodded. "Yes. Sometimes he says things he doesn't mean and, once, we had a pregnancy scare, but other than that, I'm really truly in love. Nobody's perfect."

Rose didn't know how to respond so she left it alone but tucked this information away in the back of her mind for later.

It was during this time, when the girls were seventeen and fourteen, that Rose, as the story goes, had her first very important experience. And Melody, too, found that her life would soon take a brand-new turn.

CHAPTER 12

THE UNICORN AND THE BABY

———

One day, after spending time in the library organizing recent records related to her peers, Rose decided to go for a stroll in the woods south of town beyond the line of houses. She wanted to be alone with her thoughts. As she had been organizing paperwork in the library, she couldn't keep herself from wondering how her story would have been different or reflected differently in the town's records had she been born of her mother, Marie. While all the other kids she knew had very standardized stories, hers stood out. This was something that had always set her apart, and she was usually quite used to it. But it came with its own set of downfalls.

She left the library, slipped between a couple of houses, and found a winding footpath to follow. Though the woods were largely untamed, it wasn't unheard of for people to come this way. Skilled hunters often lay in wait for deer or birds to bring back town, and the younger children often played in some of the clearings directly behind the houses. But, at the moment, no one was out in the woods except Rose.

The day was pleasant, a bright green smattering of plant life from recent rains had blossomed, the sun was out, and a small refreshing breeze smelled like what she could only imagine the world smelled like when it was just formed. It was the perfect day for Rose to contemplate her life's story.

After she had been retrieved from the island in the middle of the lake, the town had celebrated her arrival as if she had been sent from the heavens. The day was officially named Rose Day. It was the closest thing to a birthday she ever had. Every year following her mysterious appearance, the town of Zophren took the day off, as they had on the day she'd been found, to celebrate. As a child, she reveled in the adoration, but as she got older, she sometimes felt undeserving of such praise. Especially once she realized that other children didn't celebrate their birthdays the way she did.

By the time she was eight years old, she had begun to construct, in tandem with the other children, funny little one-act plays that they could reenact on the day of celebration as a way to include the others in the party and distract from herself. The first play was, as suggested by her dad, William, a simple reenactment of the day Rose had been found on the island. There was a mother, a father, a mayor, a baby doll, and everybody else who was in the play got to march as townsfolk. Everybody loved it.

But as the years went by, the story grew and grew and grew. This past year, the play was set on a stormy night, and William had to heroically swim across the lake with Rose because his boat had broken. When he arrived back onshore with the baby Rose, a mysterious rider on horseback suddenly appeared and ran off the stage calling, "Goodbye! Goodbye, little one!" And when Marie was handed the baby Rose at the end of the play, she collapsed into joyful tears while the townsfolk gathered around and began to chant.

Though Rose had begun this tradition to take away the focus from herself, it seemed to do exactly the opposite. The townsfolk were deeply impressed with the way she could lead the other children to put together a play, and as the story and Rose grew together, everybody loved her more and more. The problem was, Rose didn't see herself the way the townsfolk did. How much of the story—both told by mouth and recorded in the library records—was true? Where *had* she come from?

As she walked farther into the woods, she noticed a nice stump next to some bushes full of red berries that looked like a wild variation of raspberries. She was a little hungry, so she pulled out her skirt to make a makeshift basket and began picking. They looked perfectly plump and were deep red. She wondered why she had never seen them before in town.

Once she'd piled a good amount of berries in her skirt, she sat down on the stump and began to eat. They tasted sugary, sweet, and a little tart. As she lazily enjoyed the berries, she gazed at the trees around her and contemplated how she was different from the rest of the town and whether she would ever know the whole story of her origin. Before she knew it, the large pile of berries in her skirt had disappeared.

I guess I didn't realize how hungry I was. She rose to get some more. But as she stood, a ripple of adrenaline surged through her body and the ground moved. She tumbled onto her knees. Suddenly, she realized that her whole body felt strange, as if it was filled with a whole hive of bees. She looked at her hands and they glowed golden brown in the spotted sunlight under the trees. Though she recognized them as her own, she couldn't help but think that there was also something foreign about them, as if she were looking at them through a fog she could only describe as dreamlike. Were these *her* hands?

Suddenly, she heard the quiet echo of a single warbling note of song. It certainly didn't sound like any songbird she'd ever heard before.

Making her way carefully back to the stump, she paused once more as the note rang out a little closer. She looked around, confused by both the note and the strange new hum surging through her body, but didn't see anything. Shrugging, she realized she was thirsty, so she gathered herself up and walked toward the stream. As she moved, she kept her thoughts focused on where she wanted to go. Though a little dizzy, she felt as though if she drank some water, she might be able to clear her head a bit.

Soon she could hear the sounds of rippling water up ahead. But as she drew closer, the warbling note rang out again, this time close by. She stopped and looked around. At first, she didn't see anything and was prepared to continue walking toward the stream, but then she saw a sparkle of light glinting off something shiny. As she stood there absolutely still, everything came into focus.

There, peeking out from behind a tree just to the right of her, was a full-grown unicorn with a silver horn glimmering in the sunshine. Its coat was snow-white, and its hooves were silver like its horn. Rose stood in amazement for a whole minute as she and the unicorn looked at each other. She didn't want to move in case she scared it away, but she also desperately wanted to be closer to see more clearly. The unicorn swished its tail and let out a long warble that startled Rose so much she fell back, landing on the ground.

The unicorn came closer. As she stood up, she fell into deep purple eyes gazing at her.

"Are you—" she started but found that standing had become quite a task.

The unicorn nodded, closed its eyes, bent one knee, and bowed its head. Then it stood back up to full height and locked eyes with her again.

Though I cannot speak as you do, I can hear you as you hear me. A solemn and silky voice found its way into Rose's head. She touched her ears questioningly, but before she could form the thought into words, the unicorn responded, *Not by ear, but by heart.*

"Ah," said Rose. "You can hear me thinking?"

Yes. Come with me. Let's go for a walk. The unicorn gestured with its head. Quiet warbling notes filled Rose's head as she followed the unicorn down a partially shaded path to the stream. Curiously, Rose glanced at the berry bushes she'd eaten from, then back down at her hands. The bush looked like any other plant that might grow in the forest, but her hands had taken on a completely new appearance in the shade; somehow the backs of her hands seemed to sparkle when tiny rays of sunshine fell through the leaves above, and her nails shone like stars in the night.

"The music notes—am I the only one who can hear you?" Rose asked when they'd reached the stream, but the unicorn didn't answer.

Drink if you are thirsty. These waters are pure and will make you strong.

Rose bent down and cupped water in her hands. She was quite thirsty and drank for a long time before wiping her mouth and hands off on her skirt. Almost immediately, her head felt crystal clear. Then the unicorn gestured to her with a gentle throw of its head for her to follow. She did.

They walked in silence, going farther into the forest than Rose had ever been. The silence was filled with little humming notes that Rose supposed came from the unicorn. Whatever the case, she found that the notes calmed her.

Soon, they came to the edge of a small cliff. Off in the distance to their left, a little waterfall from the stream fell over and landed in a pond below.

All must end somewhere, the unicorn said as Rose gazed over the cliff at the pond. Beyond the pond lay another cliff; the little pond was surrounded, in fact, by an entire bowl of land.

"Do you live here?"

Yes. I knew that it was time I meet you.

"Meet me?"

You are special, Rose. You know this.

Rose temporarily forgot that the unicorn could hear her thoughts. *I am special, but I don't know where I came from or what I'm destined to do in this life. Everybody expects so much, but I am so alone.*

The unicorn moved closer and nuzzled her shoulder. *You are not alone. I know where you came from.*

Rose immediately jolted back at this response, touching her shoulder gingerly as if she'd been kissed. Then she asked the question she had pondered over her lifetime more than any other: "Where did I come from?"

First, I will tell you where I came from and where the water comes from. The unicorn moved next to the edge of the cliff, carefully sat on its haunches, then folded its forelegs beneath its body. Rose sat down adjacent and dangled her legs over the edge.

The north mountains are tall, and you know this. Snow falls in the winter, and when it melts, it follows a path down toward the lake in your town. The water eventually ends here, in this pond. My ancestors lived on the mountains long before you or your ancestors settled this area. They were in charge of carving the path for the water to follow. It will never run out because of them. They moved the rocks to catch the melting snow, and at the mouth of the lake, they built a dam to keep the lake full. The water that pools over that dam becomes the stream that you drank out of earlier, and the last of the water collects here. Under the pond is a reservoir; the ground drinks up the extra water and keeps it safe. There is a cave you can follow down in the valley that will lead you there. In times of drought, there is still water in the earth, even if no snow falls. But no humans remember.

Rose gazed out across the land as she listened, drinking up the story as if she'd never heard a better one.

When your ancestors came to claim this land, they understood that it was a paradise. They built the two bridges and settled around the lake. We unicorns had to be stealthier. In the first years of your people's settlement, many of us were killed for food. It is treachery to kill a unicorn because we can live forever and, as you now know, we are good for the land, tilling and moving it so that it can sustain life indefinitely. Many of my kind were lost. I was quite young during this time, and it was my job to sneak into the butcher's shop late at night to steal back the horns of the fallen. To most humans, we do not appear to be unicorns, especially if they are undeserving of knowing what magic we possess. We can judge human character instinctively. There were not many who deserved to know. Many thought we were deer, but still, our horns had to be retrieved. In death, the horn's magical properties do not die. Children know this. They are the only humans we cannot hide our true form from.

It was during one of these very late nights that I was in town stealing back the horns to bury on grounds far away from the town that a little girl saw me. She knew what I was, and I told her what I was doing. Though I begged her to stay and keep my secret, she ran away with me, and I raised her out here in the forest. That was one hundred years ago.

"What happened to her?" Rose asked.

She led the rest of the unicorns away to a mountain some ways from here. She thought they would be safer there, that they might be able to start over and claim new land as their own the way they had here. My brother and I remained here to watch over the forest. But after fifty years, she returned as an old lady with a grown daughter, begging for our help. More humans had come to settle, and the unicorns were in trouble. My brother went to their aid, and none of them ever returned. I heard tell from the birds that fly over all the land that the unicorns were no more, but the woman's daughter still knew the stories of the unicorns, though she kept them to herself. That is the story of the town northeast of you called Nia, which I know you barter with now and then.

Rose considered this story for a moment before asking, "So, you are the last of your kind. But do the people of Nia know of the unicorns? Because of the girl's daughter?"

Who's to say? If they do, it is only from stories. Story turns to fable, and life goes on. But yes, I am the last of my kind. If I am wise, I can live much longer, but it's a lonely life. I am all the forest has left in the ways of magic. I think you can relate to this, yes? Being the only one of your kind?

"Yes," Rose said. "But I won't live forever."

But stories can live forever. And I know a good one. Would you like to hear it?

Rose looked at the unicorn; its purple eyes sparkled pink in the sunlight.

Some seventeen years ago, something unprecedented happened. A young girl from Nia showed up at the entry bridge to Zophren in the middle of the night, her belly protruding from her coat. She could hardly walk. I found her because, like you, I could hear her thoughts churning in her head like a siren. She birthed her baby in the forest and cried and cried. I helped calm her with my magic, but still, she was distraught. She told me she knew of the unicorns, that she'd heard of them from her grandmother, and she wanted to give one last gift to us. That was why she had walked all the way from Nia to Zophren.

By that time, it was only me remaining, but I was grateful to her. She left me her baby, never told me more about the conception except that the baby was special—a gift to the town of Zophren in hopes that magic might still live here as it did before. She told me her gift was that she had stolen the evidence of unicorns, one last horn hidden in her grandmother's house so that nobody would ever believe the stories again, and I'd be free to live carefully in the woods. Though she couldn't return the land to what it once was, she hoped that the humans and the land would both be helped by a little magic. But she had lost faith in the people of Nia. They had turned greedy, she said. But for Zophren, the place where unicorns used to roam, there might still be hope. Her body was so fragile, she died soon after giving birth. Before her last breath, she gave me two dying wishes: that she be buried in an unmarked grave and that her baby be given the locket around her neck as something to remember her by.

But with her baby, I was tasked with bridging the gap between myself, the last magic remaining here, and the humans who desperately needed a reminder of how blessed their land was. I could not raise this baby the way I raised the other little girl. It would have been wrong to raise a small child away from humans when they were so near. I let the baby sleep and hold onto the last unicorn horn given to me by her mother as I figured out how to give the baby to the town. The magic from *the horn kept the baby fed as I made up my mind on what I was to do. The next night, I swaddled the baby, made sure she had her necklace, buried the unicorn horn, and delivered her in a basket to the island in the middle of the lake.*

"It was me," Rose breathed.

It was you. Your story holds power, and I think you know this.

"What am I supposed to do?" Rose looked at her hands, stained red from the berries. How could this be? Was she part of some magical forgotten history?

Establish yourself here, give your town the magic that they need. Though they don't remember the times of magic and their ancestors were too foolish to see us for what we were, humans need a touch of magic, a glimmering hope that special things do happen. You have that power, and, in fact, you have the power to restore some of the magic that has been lost.

"I do? How?"

You are not old now, but one day, you will be. And the town has given you much power to lead. Take it with grace. When droughts come, when mouths are too many, come back here to find the water, and share with your people. I will remain here, but I don't think it wise to speak with you again. You are no longer a child. I have told you all I know, and now you are ready to share your magic—something I can tell you've always known you had but never knew how to wrangle. Practice, and you'll do well.

And if you need to, you can unearth the horn that you were born with. It lies under the razzle-dazzle berries that make you feel alive. It can guide you to the water if you forget where to go. It can also perform small miracles if need be, but I do not advise this. Save it for the times you need it most.

The unicorn stood up and so did Rose. She looked long and hard into the unicorn's eyes.

"I'm not ready," Rose said.

You are ready. I'm sure of it. Will you keep my secret?

"I will," Rose said, and the unicorn closed its eyes, bowed, and turned to walk away.

Step by step, the music faded, and the unicorn disappeared behind the trees.

Dazed, Rose followed the footpath back to the stream, back to the berry bush, and as she walked, tossed the entire story the unicorn had told her around in her head. The unicorns made this place, the people were foolish, her family was from Nia, and she was in charge of the remaining magic. Was this all true? Could all of this be real? She had never heard tell of anything so outlandish, but she also couldn't deny what she had experienced. It had to be true. And maybe, just maybe, somebody had heard the hooves of the unicorn as it ran back into the forest the night it delivered her. Was that where that bit of story, the part about the mysterious rider, had come from?

When she finally reached the stump beside the razzle-dazzle berries, she sat down to take it all in. She thought briefly about having some more berries but decided against it. Her mom would be serving dinner soon. The sun was beginning to set.

Instead of digging up the unicorn horn right then and there as she was tempted, she decided to wait until she could come back.

She walked back home in the purple twilight, but when she arrived at the back of her house, Melody was waiting for her on the porch in tears. Above the roof was smoke from the fireplace, proof that dinner was already being made, and the sun was falling rapidly behind purple and orange clouds. When Rose saw her sister, she rushed to her side. Melody looked up, full of shame, and fell into Rose's arms, continuing to sob.

"What's wrong? What's happened?" Rose asked. As Melody cried uncontrollably, Rose stroked her hair. "It's okay. It's okay. I know, I know. Just tell me what's wrong."

Melody took a deep shuddering breath and sat up straight to look Rose in the eyes. Tears streamed down her cheeks, but she had a look of determination on her face, as if she were willing herself to stop crying long enough to tell Rose the news.

"It's Silverton. He and I are…" Melody started. "We're going to have a baby. I haven't told anyone yet."

At this, Rose's eyes widened in disbelief, and Melody dissolved into more tears. Rose's mystical afternoon crashed down around her. She comforted her sister and silently worried whether Melody, but especially her boyfriend Silverton, were ready.

CHAPTER 13

MOTHER MERMAID

——

After a few days passed, and it had become clear to Rose that Melody wasn't going to talk about the pregnancy, she decided to take things into her own hands. Although Rose had secrets to keep, she also had magic to share.

"I'm bored," Rose whispered to Melody who was sitting on the pew next to her during a town meeting. "Wanna go for a walk?"

Melody agreed. They slipped out the back door as quietly as they could. Rose strode confidently down the path. She knew today was the perfect day to show her sister what she'd discovered on her own the other day—the magical wonder that she'd known. She was hoping that, by sharing the magic of the razzle-dazzle berries, which must have been fueled by the unicorn horn in the soil underneath them, she could help her sister find some purpose or at least gain some clarity. She knew she wouldn't see the unicorn again, but she thought that if there was a miracle she needed, it was to help Melody begin planning for the baby's arrival.

"Where are we going?" Melody asked, taking up a steady jog to keep up with Rose's pace.

"You'll see." Rose smiled.

They strode across the bridge and followed the path around the lake toward the housing neighborhood. The day was bright and cool, but an electricity in the air hinted at approaching rain. Melody was curious as to where they were going yet had a feeling she was about to risk getting in trouble.

"Are we going into the forest?" Melody asked as Rose turned down a narrow path in between two houses.

"Yep. I found some yummy berries out here. You've gotta try them."

"Oh!" said Melody. "Really? I thought you were taking me to where you've been hiding those stolen library books."

Rose laughed. "You'll never find the place."

Melody joined in, laughing, "Oh, someday, I will!"

As they turned a corner east, the path grew narrow until they were simply climbing over branches in a direction that only Rose seemed to be sure of. Finally, they could hear the gentle rambling of the river ahead.

"You have seriously got to try these berries. I call them razzle-dazzle berries," Rose said.

Melody laughed. "Show me the razzle-dazzle berries!"

Rose set off southbound along the line of the riverbank, then stopped at a bush teetering toward the edge of the bank.

"Here they are," she said and began picking them. They were bright, juicy red. The girls ate berry after berry until finally, chins red from the juice, they wandered back to the sitting log, both in a stupor from so much sugary fruit all at once.

"I feel funny," Melody said as she sat down gingerly on the log. "As if I were filled with bubbles."

"I have to tell you something," Rose said solemnly.

Melody's eyes widened.

"I've eaten these berries before, and I think they're magical."

"What? What do you mean?"

"I mean, they showed me things I've never seen before."

Melody stared at her sister. She was starting to feel dizzy. "You what?"

Rose gazed out over the river and sighed. "I don't know. Never mind. What I really want to talk about is the baby and what you're going to do about it."

Melody was still trying to regain control over the bubbly feeling in her body. Unable to process what Rose had said, Melody just smiled. Had she fallen asleep at the City Hall? Maybe she was just really tired and needed a nap. Though her sister Rose seemed calm, serene almost, she felt as if she'd been thrown into a dreamlike trance and was beginning to feel a little queasy.

They sat there in silence as Rose waited for a response to her question while Melody focused on readjusting herself to the inescapable feeling of experiencing a particularly vivid dream.

Finally, Melody turned to Rose and asked, "What do you think it's like, being a mother?"

"I don't know," said Rose slowly. As her eyes wandered over the tree branches in search of a longer answer, something in the water splashed. Both girls jumped in surprise. A great ripple emerged from the middle of the lake. Then the head of an old woman with long silvery hair popped out of the water. They screamed.

The woman in the water had wrinkled skin, yet it seemed sturdy—as if there were something stronger holding it tight. She smiled gently at them and waited patiently for the initial shock to wear off. The old woman rose a little higher out of the water to reveal her nakedness, and they both stared.

"I've been expecting you two," the woman said. "There are secrets in the water, and the waters from the mountain have told me of you."

Melody looked at Rose uneasily.

"Swim with me," the woman said. "You have eaten the berries so you can breathe as I breathe."

She sank back into the water and as she dove, a large tail splashed water on them.

Melody whispered to Rose, "Is she a… mermaid?"

Rose giggled. "Looks like it, come on." She shed her shoes and dress as Melody stood dumbfounded beside her. The mermaid raised her head again somewhere in the middle of the river.

"Don't be scared, child. No harm will befall you. Come with me. I have much to tell you."

Reluctantly, Melody followed suit and stripped. The girls waded into the water. Rose peeked over at Melody's stomach to see if it was protruding at all yet but Melody, feeling her eyes, said aloud, "Not yet, but soon."

Rose nodded. "We'll figure it out."

When they met the mermaid in the middle of the river, she smiled at them and said, "Trust that you can breathe as I breathe. And follow me."

The girls shrugged and, after watching the mermaid dive, they followed suit. The water felt cool and refreshing. Melody took her first breath underwater and laughed.

She grabbed Rose's shoulder as they swam and moved her mouth, but only bubbles came out. Rose took her first breath and laughed, too. They could breathe, but they couldn't speak.

As they swam behind the mermaid, they wondered at the green plants growing up from the bottom of the riverbed and the smooth white rocks that littered the shallows on either side. Fish of all sizes and colors swam past, as if unaware that two humans had dropped into their world for a swim.

After what felt like a blink of an eye, they reached the dam and swam over it into the lake. The mermaid kept swimming without regard to whether they followed or not. They did their best to keep up. The lake was considerably deeper than the river, and it grew dark toward the bottom. Soon, though, as they swam over the deep darkness, they came to the island.

The mermaid guided them around the eastern side of the island to a cave that led into the island itself. Once inside, they followed twists and turns before coming to a small cove where light shone in. There seemed to be a small pond on the island they'd never seen before that led to this underwater cave. They came up to the surface to find three rocks, warm from the sun. The mermaid sat on one, and the two girls followed suit.

"Nobody remembers this little cove," the mermaid explained, "and no human remembers magic anymore, at least not here in Zophren."

Melody reached for Rose's hand. When Rose looked at her, Melody made a confused face as if to confirm that they were somehow having the same hallucination. Rose gave her sister an encouraging nod. "Why don't you ask her something?" Rose whispered and squeezed Melody's hand.

"Why were you expecting us?" Melody asked. She was naked, wet from swimming in the river, and in the presence of an ancient mermaid. Nothing was making sense.

"There was a prophecy told long ago when the magic on the mountain flowed down more readily. It said that there would be two sisters, one with magic herself and one with the gift of a water babe."

"A water babe?" Melody asked.

"The last hope that magic can be restored to these waters. In years to come, the snow on the mountain will disappear and no water will reach this lake. The water will stagnate, and many could lose their lives. The sister with magic will know where to find the clean water, and the water babe will be able to deliver it."

Rose sat silently. She thought about asking the ancient mermaid about the unicorn. It, too, had talked about the water—even told her where to find clean water in the reservoir under the pond at the end of the river. But she kept silent. She didn't want to break her promise.

"Let me get this straight," Melody said. "I'm the sister who will have the water babe because obviously, I'm the pregnant sister, so that means that Rose is the sister with magic, right?"

"That's correct." The mermaid smiled.

Melody frowned. "How is Rose magic?"

The mermaid waved her hand at Rose as if to encourage her to speak.

"Remember the berries we ate?" Rose said to her sister. "They're magic, just like I told you. We have magic that we can use if there's ever a crisis."

Melody didn't say anything at all, so the mermaid turned to Rose.

"I saw you the other day at the same spot down the river," she said. "Though I am pleased to see you and your sister, you must be wise with the berries that grow in the forest there. Their roots reach the water so they are clean, but they must not be abused."

Rose nodded solemnly. It had been her wish to help her sister find clarity about the pregnancy the way she had found clarity about the circumstances of her birth, but maybe the razzle-dazzle berries were more powerful than she'd thought. She glanced over at her sister who was in deep thought.

"Don't you think we should head home?" Melody finally asked.

Rose agreed and got up from the rock she'd been sitting on. The mermaid moved toward the water and, as she did, her breasts swayed.

"One last thing," the mermaid said as she eased her tail back into the water. "I have a gift for you." She reached down toward her belly where flesh turned to fish and plucked two silvery scales. Holding them out so the girls could take them, she said, "Each scale has the power to grant wishes. All you must do is hold the scale and focus on your wish. The wishes will not run out. But I must also warn you of this power. If used in excess, you may find that you wish to have no more wishes but cannot find the will to stop. Like the berries, you must find a balance, or else you'll go mad."

Rose took one scale from the mermaid's hands, but Melody hesitated.

"Are you sure?" she asked.

"Yes," said the mermaid. "You will soon be a mother of a very important water babe. If ever you need what you can't find, you will have this scale to wish upon. It is my gift to you that you may protect your town from the drought when you are old."

"The drought?" asked Melody.

"You are young now, but you will not always be so. You'll know what to do then, don't worry." With that, the mermaid pressed the remaining scale into Melody's hand and slipped into the water. The girls silently followed, each turning over this information in their heads as they swam back to the part of the river past the dam where they'd left their clothing.

When the mermaid delivered them to the spot, she merely asked, "Will you keep my secret so that I may continue to live in these waters?"

"We will," said Rose, but Melody was already fetching her clothes from the bank. The mermaid disappeared under the water, and the girls began to dry off and get dressed.

"I don't know about you," said Melody, as she turned over the mermaid scale in her hand, "but I really want to go home now."

"But aren't we going to talk about the pregnancy and what you're going to do?"

"We were, but I don't know what's gotten into you. You're coming out to the forest and eating these berries and seeing weird beings and believing in magic and—" Melody shifted uncomfortably.

"I believe that we are something special," said Rose quietly. "I didn't mean to scare you, I just wanted to share the magic with you."

"Well, thanks, I guess. But I need to go home now. I have to figure out how I'm going to tell our parents about this baby, but I don't think I'm going to use the term 'water babe.' I can't even tell if that mermaid was real or if those berries just made us fall into some weird dream state."

"I'm sorry," Rose said, but before she could think of more to say, Melody handed over her mermaid scale and marched off toward home.

CHAPTER 14

THE FAMILY GROWS

———

Once Melody got up the courage to tell her parents she was pregnant, she unknowingly set off a chain of events in which William and Marie's family expanded exponentially. But with the joy of new additions also came loss.

William took the news of Melody's unexpected pregnancy well. It surprised her because she had wondered if her dad even liked the boy she'd been seeing. Marie, however, reacted exactly as Rose had predicted: she began with reprimands and ended with tears.

"It's a surprise," William told Marie after Melody had left the house. "But it's still a blessing. You'll see." And despite Marie's worry that her daughter was too young to be having a child of her own, William set about making plans for his first grandchild.

With the help of some men from town, along with a few young men training as builder apprentices, William built a small house behind the original home. "You'll want your own place now that you'll have a family," William told Melody. She excitedly began making plans for how she would decorate inside once it was done.

After growing up in Rose's shadow, Melody basked in all of the attention now paid to her by the town. She liked being the center of the traditional procession toward City Hall and hearing the chant for her baby. She glowed like an angel on the day of her wedding, when she was adorned with flowers and given gifts for both the baby and their new home. With all the celebration, she finally felt confident that her life was moving in the right direction.

Silverton put a damper on all the good news. He seemed to constantly be grumbling over things like how their house ought to have been built bigger or that Melody's moods were too much for him to handle or that he didn't like sacrificing time with his friends to build a crib or decorate the baby's room. Melody frequently vented to Rose about his various complaints.

"I can't tell if the pregnancy is making me nutty or if Silverton is actually a jerk," she told Rose one day.

Unsure how to respond—especially because she worried that she knew the answer—Rose did her best to reassure her sister. "I'm sure he's just nervous about being a father. Try not to overthink it."

When the baby was born, Silverton finally showed his true colors. As Melody went into labor late one fall night and the women disappeared into the back bedroom of the new house to guide her, he slipped out the front door, promising William he'd be right back. But the neighbors saw him on the road out of town, bags packed, never to return. By morning, everybody in Zophren knew.

When Melody asked where he was after the baby arrived in the middle of the night, when the owls were still hooting, William assured her that he would be right back. Melody decided to wait until he returned to name their baby. But by morning, when the neighbors began showing up on the porch to quietly inform William and Marie of what had happened, William had to bury his anger and gather the courage to tell Melody.

Melody cried until she couldn't open her eyes anymore. Rose took the baby girl, who remained without a name for the first few days, and their parents paced between the houses nervously, unsure how to celebrate and mourn at the same time.

"I don't want her all alone with her baby in this new house," Marie told William, who agreed. As Melody lay in bed alternating between sleeping and crying, William spent his time moving everything but Melody and the baby back into her childhood room in the big house. Marie gathered up all of Silverton's belongings—even the decorations on the wall for fear they would remind her daughter of her marriage cut short—and sold them all in town. Rose focused on the baby and her sister.

"You'll be better off without him," Rose soothed her. But it took Melody a week before she was ready to get out of bed and greet her newborn, a baby girl she decided to name Nicole.

The new house behind William and Marie's sat empty while Melody raised her baby with help from her parents and sister. For the first several months, the mood was tense as Melody cycled between the joy of holding her beautiful baby and the heartbreak of being abandoned by her husband. For months, she couldn't face leaving the house.

But then their household had some unexpected luck. Rose fell in love that year, just as Melody was beginning to think less of what she'd lost and more about the joys of her new baby.

One day, a man ten years Rose's senior delivered new books to the library from Nia. After spending the afternoon sorting and categorizing together, comparing their tastes in literature, and flirting as only librarians can, they'd kissed and promised to see each other again.

His name was Zachary, though he went by Zach, and he had served as a librarian in Nia for quite some time. Rose fell in love fast. And it certainly helped that Zach brought her as many unicorn stories as he could find since Nia had the best collection of them. Zach, for his part, was smitten.

"It's like I'm dating the town celebrity," he often teased her. "Which isn't normal for a girl who likes books so well."

And after four months of visiting, on Rose Day when the town threw their yearly celebration, Zach got down on one knee after the play and asked Rose to marry him. She said yes, and the whole town celebrated late into the night.

The next morning, Rose took Melody aside and asked, "Would it be okay if Zach and I lived in the house Dad built for you?"

"I don't see anything wrong with you having the house," Melody said. "I definitely don't want it. I'm just nervous that you and Zach are getting married so quickly."

"I know," said Rose. "But I've never felt this way before. It has to be love."

Soon after, a second wedding overtook the town. This time, there was a parade and an extended play of Rose's life to go along with it. Zach promised the townsfolk one by one as they came up to meet him that he would take the best care he possibly could of Rose. He assured them he knew how special she was.

They moved into the little house, and Melody was glad to see it gain happy new memories instead of rot with all her broken dreams inside. Rose got pregnant almost immediately and waddled around the library until she was finally convinced to spend the last month of her pregnancy at home getting things ready for her new arrival. Melody was ever helpful since, for once, she could offer Rose advice on experiences she had been through first. She was also excited to think about their babies being close in age.

"After a few years, they'll be best friends," she told Rose. How could they not? They would share the yard between the two houses.

Zach stayed for the entire duration of labor, which was both a testament to his patience—for it was an especially long and arduous process for Rose—and a testament to William's determination not to let this one out of his sight, lest he follow Silverton's path.

Finally, a baby girl made her entrance, wailing so loudly William was reminded of the cries he'd heard on the island that morning long ago. Upon making sure that Zach had made it into the bedroom to see his new baby, William snuck outside to shed quiet, happy tears before meeting the new addition. They all crowded round in wonder at the tiny baby, and Rose whispered weakly, "Her name will be Anne."

For a time, the expanded family lived in their two adjacent houses happily. But when Melody's daughter, Nicole, was six and Rose's daughter, Anne, was five, disaster struck again.

One dry and biting winter night, Zach had returned from a long journey distributing books that were overstocked in Zophren's library. His travels had taken him far beyond the usual two towns nearest Zophren, as all three libraries had very similar collections apart from the works that were specifically dedicated to their community histories.

Weary and cold from the trip back to Zophren, he arrived home late in the night and crawled into bed with Rose.

"Hey, honey, I missed you," she murmured and adjusted to the stinging coldness of his skin against her own warm body.

"I missed you too," he sighed before kissing her. And they fell asleep, happy to be in the same bed together.

But when Rose woke in the morning, she found him dead in the bed beside her, his blue lips still in a faint smile.

Her scream that morning was the second time in her life that she woke the whole town.

Melody and Nicole ran out of the big house and met her at her front door where she stood shaking and in tears with Anne on her hip. The children were taken to the lake to swim while the two sisters mourned together the loss of a second husband. A funeral followed, and soon after that, Melody and Nicole moved into the little house with Rose and Anne, which is how the two sisters and two cousins lived for a great many years.

* * *

The two cousins, Nicole and Anne, grew up like sisters. They argued, shared dresses, told secrets, then argued some more. For both Melody and Rose, it was a relief to share parenting responsibilities equally. And though they often laughed at their strangely pieced together family, raising their daughters together bonded them in a way they had never bonded before. Their daughters, they were sure, were lucky to have each other because Rose and Melody knew that someday their daughters would be just as close as they were.

As it turned out, Nicole took after her aunt Rose in personality and Anne took after her aunt Melody. Nicole had never known her father, so the only big events she remembered were the day her uncle died and moving from the big house to the little house. Though Marie had insisted that there was no reason for Melody and Nicole to move out to the little house with Rose and Anne, Melody wanted some space, even if it was just a small yard, between herself and her mom's unpredictable dark moods. Though she'd grown up soothing her mom, sharing the pain of Silverton leaving with her was overwhelming. Marie seemed to dwell on it at times, but Melody wanted to put it in the past.

Plus, Melody rationalized, Rose needed her and, whether she would admit it or not, she needed Rose, too. It just made sense.

Melody's daughter, Nicole, did not share these sentiments. She preferred to follow her Grandma Marie around. On the days Marie didn't get out of bed, Nicole would help around the big house the way Melody did as a child because, truly, it was the house she wished to stay in. Marie was better for this arrangement; Nicole was a cheerful child, and Marie couldn't stay down for long with her around.

Anne, on the other hand, remembered snippets of her dad, Zach, and the day he died was seared vividly in her memory. Having a dad and then losing him was much harder on her than it was for Nicole to have never known her father. Like her Aunt Melody, Anne was also reluctant to fall prey to believing the stories full of magic that her mom told her. With death such a familiar thing, she couldn't fathom the hope her mom's stories focused on. Though her mom would wink at the end of her tales about unicorns and mermaids, Anne viewed them as fairy tales and didn't understand why her mom was so intent on telling such wild fantasies. She chalked it up to her mother spending too much time getting stuck in books. As Anne grew older, Rose stopped telling her these stories and began to wonder if they might only be remembered dreams. And she didn't dare ask her sister; Melody had never spoken another word about it after they'd met the mermaid.

As far as social status, Rose's yearly parade continued. Melody, by this time, had not only gotten over the lavishness of this event but had begun recruiting the children to carry on the tradition of the one-act play.

Nicole soon became the star who played Rose's character—she was confident and cheery in disposition, the way Rose had been as a child. Anne, however, preferred the steady work of building the backdrops, helping with costumes, and, in general, making sure she was never picked for an acting role.

Rose wasn't terribly bothered by this. Like her daughter, she too sometimes felt a little disillusioned with the fanfare. Though she had grown used to the ridiculousness of the yearly celebration, she did her best to let the townsfolk have what they wanted. Like the unicorn had said, if she let the town believe in the magic, she was granted a leadership position in the town by default, which was useful to have every once in a while. And when it came to the library, she flourished as she always had and became well-respected in the town for the way she organized library events and ran things. Despite these successes, she found it easy to keep her ego reined in, especially when it came to the stories that both her sister and daughter simply didn't believe.

As the years went by, Nicole and Anne grew into people who both surprised and confused their moms. Though they outgrew their childish yelling matches, their different personalities were like night and day, and they often didn't understand each other. Nicole became engrossed in establishing her status, which made her haughty at times, and Anne liked to think that she was morally superior to her cousin because she didn't parade around the town pretending to like people when she didn't.

"I really thought they were going to be best friends," Melody told Rose sadly one day as they listened to their daughters argue in the next room.

"I know," Rose said. "It's funny how they've turned out. Nicole so much like me and Anne so much like you, yet they can't get along."

"Oh, but they're certainly their own people, too," Melody said with a sigh and nodded toward the other room where the girls were loudly disagreeing over outfits.

As the cousins got older, their lives continued to diverge as much as was possible in a small lake community. Whatever little resentments they had toward each other were never explicitly brought to the forefront, but their moms knew that somehow, despite their dreams, their daughters simply didn't get along.

Nicole went on to lead many of the children's activities in the town with the guidance and support of her mom. At age seventeen, she fell in love with the butcher's son, Landon, a strong young man who was quite charismatic and went on to become an important member of the town council at the impressively early age of twenty. He and Nicole married, had two boys—Michael and Ernest—and built a house on the southwest corner of the neighborhood, where the road curved around the lake toward town. They became a very prominent family and, as the years went by, made less and less time for the rest of the extended family, save Nicole's mom, Melody.

Anne wasn't far behind her cousin and began dating a quiet young man named Frank who delivered the mail around town. They kept to themselves and dated for a couple of years before Rose finally nudged them toward marriage. Soon, they had a daughter who was born with a little brown birthmark on her shoulder that looked like a button. They told the townsfolk at her naming ceremony that her name was Bella but mostly they called her Button. They weren't as involved in town goings-on as Nicole and Landon. Instead, they seemed content to live in a small house near the road that led out of town. Rose was the only one who visited regularly.

William, by the time his three great-grandchildren had all arrived, was officially an elder, free of town duty for the rest of his life. And it was a good thing. Both he and Marie were beginning to have more trouble getting around and began to stay home more often than not. Though Rose and Melody didn't like to see the decline, they used it to their advantage. Nicole and Anne's children didn't see much of each other. The one way they were able to wrangle the whole family together was for Saturday night dinners with the elderly couple. Rose and Melody dragged their daughters and their daughters' husbands and children to these dinners without fail, in hopes of keeping the family together.

William reported to his daughters in quiet asides at these dinners that their mom seemed to be doing well.

"But just in case, keep bringing over those kids. They help."

His daughters would laugh and promise to keep bringing their children and grandchildren. For them, weekly dinners were the best way to keep up a sense of family unity despite Nicole and Anne's reluctance.

William and Marie both passed away when their great-grandchildren hit their early teen years. William fell ill first, then Marie, and before anyone knew it, they had died within hours of each other—a true lovers' death.

The funeral was a week-long affair. Zophren had lost one of its best historians and most accomplished cooks, not to mention the esteemed parents of Rose, the baby from the island and a full-fledged mythical piece of town history. In honor of their achievements, the town named the library after William and everybody pitched in the recipes Marie had made them over the years to compile a town cookbook.

Afterward, Rose spent a great deal of time going through the big house and all its contents, though Melody went back and forth between mourning in the little house and visiting Nicole. Rose tried to convince Anne to come help her sort through William and Marie's belongings, but Anne had a lot more than on her plate than she could handle.

As it turned out, Anne's daughter, Button, was the second fantastical addition to Zophren—one that even Rose herself wasn't prepared for.

CHAPTER 15

BELLA BUTTON

———

Button was a lively child from the moment she exited her mother's womb. She climbed out of her crib, got into her mom's cabinets, asked "why" incessantly, and threw full-body fits to get her way. From the get-go, she was a handful. Anne and her husband, Frank, didn't quite know what to do with her. Their temperaments were both quiet and steady, so to have a daughter who so defiantly questioned and often wrecked the world around her had them at a loss. But she was bright and beautiful, so they did their best to keep up.

Button was seventeen years old when her great-grandparents, William and Marie, passed away. For the most part, she'd grown into a cheerful and curious girl who excelled in her studies and ran around town with the boys her age. She might have run around with her two cousins, Ernest and Michael, but they were on the opposite side of town. And she got the feeling quite often that her Aunt Nicole wouldn't like it if they associated.

Button was practically always in trouble, but it wasn't the kind of trouble that made folks shake their heads. She was more likely to pull pranks, stay out too late, wander too far into the forest, or ask questions about things her mom didn't want to answer.

One evening, shortly after the last of her great-grandparents' funeral proceedings, Rose, Button's grandmother, showed up on their doorstep unexpectedly.

Button had always had an affinity for her grandmother, but besides the weekly family gatherings, her mom arranged visits less and less as Button got older. When Button was little, Rose would come visit the house during the day more often. It was during these visits that Button and Rose built their bond. While her mom and dad worked, Button would beg to hear the stories of Rose's beginning on the island and the fantastical tales that Rose would tell straight from the town's history book. They liked to play pretend together and take long strolls on the edges of town in the forest, the mountain trails, and the lake.

When Rose showed up that evening, though, she looked disheveled and tired. Anne invited her inside, and they sat in the living room. Button was sitting on the floor painting. She had recently gotten it in her head that nobody ever cared to paint floors and that was something she wanted to fix. Her mother had practically given up on telling her what she could and could not do. Anne wanted to pick her battles wisely. There would come a day, she thought, that a battle would come up that she would need to win. Painting the floor wasn't one of them.

"Are you okay, Mama?" asked Anne.

"Yes," sighed Rose. "I'm just tired and needed a break from cleaning out your grandparents' house. You wouldn't believe the amount of stuff packed in there. And, of course, I got stuck in your grandfather's library trying to sort things." She smiled at Button painting the floor. "I think Button would like some of the stories I've found."

"Mama," said Anne. "No offense, but those stories would probably give Button some bad ideas."

"Nonsense. I know you think all the stories I tell and the stories your grandfather told are silly, but stories are important. They help us figure out who we are and what we're supposed to do."

"You know how I feel about it, is all. Don't go convincing her that unicorns are real."

But at the dissent from her mom, Button perked up. "I'll help you, Grandma Rose. I could come stay a few days and keep you company."

Anne frowned, but Rose smiled. "That would be wonderful, love. We just have to get your mother's permission."

But just as Rose and Button began to pout and beg Anne for permission, Frank walked in the door.

"Good to see you, Rose. How are you?" he asked.

"Doing well, thanks," Rose beamed. "I was just asking Anne here if it would be alright if I borrowed your daughter to help me clean out my parents' house."

Button splashed paint at her father's feet. "Yeah," she piped up. "I'd be out of your hair long enough for my floor art to dry."

Frank looked at the floor, currently a half-finished abstract design of colorful curves and loops, now with splatters of yellow at his feet. He sighed and gave Anne a little helpless shrug.

"Alright," Anne gave in. "But take the paint with you!"

* * *

When she arrived at the big house in the morning, Button found Rose laying on her back in the front room, gazing at the ceiling amidst several piles of books and paperwork. Though she was teetering on the brink of old age, Rose had remained remarkably spry—probably due to lifting heavy books at the library and her insistent exploration of the forest and mountains. As Button walked in, Rose arose to greet her.

"How can I help?" Button asked, hugging her grandma and looking around the room. There really *was* a whole library there. She wasn't sure how all of it would fit in the little library downtown. Then again, maybe it could.

"Well," said Rose. "I've already attempted to begin sorting genres." She pointed at the various piles. "This pile is town historical records, this is folklore, and this is standard literature that can either go in our library or be shipped out to one of our neighboring towns. I was thinking you could help with the historical records. I know you've always liked fantastic stories, and there are some wild ones in here."

"Yeah?"

"Oh, yeah. I found one just a couple minutes ago about how a boy had once climbed up the mountain as far as he could to try and find where the river began." Rose walked in between the piles before coming to the folklore. "While he was up there, though, he began to have visions that he described as the rainbow, but brighter and with more colors. The record says it rained on him up there, but his account doesn't say anything at all about it." She pulled a book out of the stack and handed it to Button. "Here it is. When he finally came down from the mountain, he swore to everyone who would listen that our souls rise up and get stuck in the clouds that hang over those mountains and when it rains, the pieces of our souls that have gotten stuck rain back down on us."

"Whoa," Button said. "I remember when I was little, and you would tell me stories. They always made me feel like this town is surrounded by magic."

"It is, love." Rose smiled.

"I haven't seen it." Button snorted. "I like the stories and all, but my mom says they're all just fantasy. Dreams that we like to pretend are real."

"Your mom was never very amused with the stories I told," Rose sighed. "But I don't think it matters if you think they're real or not. Even if they *are* pretend, there are things we can learn from them. Take the one about the boy. Whether or not the rain actually contains little bits of the souls of our loved ones, water circulates forever. It's one of those things about life that never changes. It snows on the mountain, the water falls down, it collects in the lake, some of it evaporates into the clouds, and it starts all over again."

"Yeah, so? What does the water cycle have to do with rainbow visions and bits of soul?"

"It's just a dreamy way of looking at death," Rose said. "If parts of our souls continue to live on and help those who live after us grow, then there's more meaning in our lives."

Button parsed this. While she thought, Rose got up and pulled more books off the shelf to sort. Flipping through them one by one, she started piling them up.

"So, you don't really believe in the magic, you just like the way the stories interpret real life?" Button finally asked.

"Oh, I believe in magic." Rose smiled mysteriously. "But I understand that seeing is believing. You'll just have to trust me on this one."

"I most certainly won't. If there's magic, I want you to show me."

Rose laughed. "Let's get through these books first, then I'll show you. But only once we've finished."

Button pulled down her own pile of books to begin sorting. "We might need a wheelbarrow to get all of this stuff to the library."

"Definitely," said Rose. "That can be your job."

They sorted through books and stories and ledgers for the next few days, always pausing to share interesting findings with each other. Button employed some of her friends to help with transporting the books to the library, and they spent a couple of days after that putting things up, organizing records, and putting together packages of what could be sent out to other libraries.

By the end of their project, Button and Rose were completely exhausted and vowed to spend an entire day floating around on the lake to unwind. For Rose, the work was highly emotional. She finally had to dedicate an entire shelf in the library toward the various histories and accounts of when she was discovered on the island and all the yearly celebrations that followed. Button, on the other hand, curious as she was, enjoyed reading up on the town gossip, finding eccentric stories, and wondering aloud at why her Grandma Rose seemed to crop up everywhere.

As they floated around the lake in a small boat after a job well done, Button began with all the questions about Rose's birth story. She had a knack for asking so many questions that it was sometimes exhausting, but Rose loved it. She remembered being just as curious at that age.

"Grandma Rose?" asked Button as she dipped her fingers in the water. "Did you mean it when you said you would show me the magic after we were done?"

"Yes," said Rose. "And we can start on the island. Row us over, will you?"

Button rowed them toward the island and pulled the little boat toward shore to tie it onto the tree branch nearest the water. She helped Rose out onto the rocky beach.

"My favorite spot is just up here." Button pointed toward a little footpath that led to the tree of baskets. Over the years, people had begun leaving little baskets with blankets and trinkets to pay homage toward Rose's mysterious arrival. It started when William left the basket where he found it so that he would always remember where he'd found Rose, but it soon turned into a good luck charm for soon-to-be parents. They would weave baskets, hang them on the tree, and—as the superstition went—if the basket was empty after a week, the couple would soon have a baby. Baskets with small, shiny trinkets were deemed the luckiest. After all, Rose had been found with a blanket and the gold locket around her neck.

The tradition had been going on so long, some of the baskets were falling apart.

"Weird, isn't it?" Rose mused. "I've always wondered where the trinkets go."

"Really?" asked Button. "I know where they go."

"You do?" Rose was surprised. "Where?"

Button grinned. "They go where I put them." She beckoned Rose to follow her farther onto the island until she came to a sudden stop. "I fell in here once. If you don't know where it is, you can hardly see it." She stepped gingerly down into a patch of plant life. "It looks like solid ground, but the vines cover up this hole. Don't worry, though. I put a ladder in, I'll show you."

Button disappeared underneath the vines while Rose watched curiously until Button popped her head up.

"Just trust me," said Button and guided her grandmother beneath the ground. As she climbed down, Rose found herself surprised that there was so much light filtering through the vines.

Once inside, Rose looked around. There were paintings on the wall of the cave. Button pointed to a corner just next to where the ladder was propped up. There was a little shelf in the cave wall full of shiny trinkets.

Rose laughed. "How long have you been stealing these?"

"A few years. Funny enough, I think someone did it before me. I wasn't the first one to put stuff on that rock over there."

"Hmm," said Rose. The cave seemed to lead off beyond the little hole. "You explored the rest of this cave?"

"Some. Not all," answered Button.

"Want to?"

"Let's go."

They followed it for a bit, adjusting to the dark and feeling their way through, but after a few minutes, Rose thought maybe they should turn back. They hadn't brought a lamp. Button wasn't so keen on turning back but was just about to agree with her grandmother when they both saw a ray of sunlight up ahead.

Both curious, they pressed forward to see where the cave let out. As they got closer, they could hear the sounds of water dripping and rippling, and Rose suddenly knew what they'd found.

"Button," she said suddenly. "Let me go ahead of you. I think I've been here before."

Button flattened herself against the wall to let Rose pass.

Sure enough, there lay the cove of rounded rocks in a little pool of water. Rays of sunshine from above still warmed them. Rose half hoped that the ancient mermaid she and Melody once talked with would reappear. Nothing of the sort happened.

"Sit," Rose said to Button. "Do you remember the story I told you about the mermaid?"

"The one that my great-aunt Melody thinks you're kind of crazy for telling?"

"Yes," said Rose. "We were actually by the river in the forest beyond the dam when we met that mermaid, but she led us here and gave us each our own little mermaid scale."

Button looked around. "Do you still have the scales?"

"Not here," Rose said. "I buried them."

They sat in silence on the warm rocks for a moment. Button peered into the shallow pool of water, noting that there was indeed what looked like an underwater tunnel that might lead out toward the lake. But what she saw just inside the lip of that tunnel took her breath away.

"Grandma? Is that… a mermaid tail?" She pointed. Silvery flecks of scales were fluttering around almost out of sight under the water.

Rose looked. "There's only one way to find out," she said and began stripping. Button didn't quite know how to react to this. She had never seen her grandmother without all her clothes on. But as Rose finished stripping, she simply looked at Button and asked, "Are you coming or not?"

Quickly, Button shed her clothes and waded in. Rose sank under the water and swam to the bottom toward the cove's exit. Button followed. It didn't take them long to get the extra perspective they needed underwater to see what was really shining at the bottom of the pool.

Stretched out—as if she'd been napping on the pool's floor—were the decaying remains of a very old mermaid. Though much of her body had deteriorated, there remained a fully intact skeleton and a few scales left shining through the dirt.

Button put her hand on Rose's arm; they both stopped swimming to take in the sight. She could hardly believe what she was seeing, but somehow, the proof of her grandma's stories soothed her. At least she could trust one person in the world to answer her questions truthfully. When Rose looked at her, Button made gestures as if to ask if they could pick up the remains and bring them up to the sitting rocks.

Rose shook her head but reached down and picked up a scale before turning to swim back up to the surface. Button surfaced after her and watched as her grandmother gently placed the scale on one of the sitting rocks before hoisting herself up out of the water.

"Do you remember what the mermaid told us about the scales?"

"They're magic," said Button, and she dove back down to the mermaid. She proceeded to gather every scale she could before swimming back up to the surface to dump her treasure on a sitting rock.

"Bella Button," Rose chided. "You do not need that many mermaid scales."

"Why not? It's endless wishes," Button argued.

"Yes, but she warned against abuse. She said to use them carefully."

"I'll put them somewhere safe, don't worry," said Button as she climbed out of the water. "I might grab one of the baskets off the tree to carry them home."

Rose frowned. "I think it would be best if you only took one, love. The wishes are endless, even with just one."

"Aw, come on, Grandma. These are really cool. You should at least take one to put it in the museum."

"I don't know, maybe," Rose said. "Why don't you leave the rest of them where you've been hiding the trinkets? That way you know where they are, and you won't have to carry them all home."

"Are you just worried about me making too many wishes? Did *you* ever make a wish?"

Startled by this question, Rose paused. "You know, I never did. I buried my mermaid scale with the unicorn horn and put them both to rest long ago."

"Well then," said Button with finality. "If you never made your own wish, you can't lecture me about it. You don't even know if it would work or not."

Rose sighed. "Just be careful."

"I will."

They left the cave and headed back toward the neighborhood across the lake. Button left all the mermaid scales where her grandma had suggested, with the pile of trinkets from the baskets, though Rose noticed that Button had put them as far back on the shelf as she could and covered them. She suspected that Button would be back there soon to claim her hoard, but, as Button had pointed out, she didn't really know what would or wouldn't happen with so many scales. And really, what was the worst that could happen?

Once they had docked, Rose told Button she would walk her home.

"You've been so much help to me, and I'm really glad we got to go on that little adventure of ours," she said with a twinkle in her eye. "Of course, this is one adventure that your mom is probably better off not knowing about."

Button seemed to be deep in thought.

"What's on your mind, dear?" Rose asked.

"I was just wondering where you buried the unicorn horn. I would really like to see it," she responded.

"Oh, it's buried under a razzle-dazzle berry bush in the forest south of town, near a sitting stump where the creek runs by. I don't think I could give you directions, but I could walk you there."

"Can we go?" asked Button. They were just passing Marie and William's house, and Button looked longingly at the trail that led into the forest behind the smaller house.

"Not today," Rose said. "We've already had quite the adventure, it's getting late, and I'm not as young as I used to be. I need to go home and sleep."

Button began to pull a face. Especially with Rose who doted on her so freely, she wasn't used to being told no so much, and this made twice in one day.

"Oh, stop it," Rose teased. "We'll go another day. Okay?"

"When?"

"Soon."

But soon wasn't soon enough for Button. The next day, she pranced into the woods with a shovel and followed the creek until she found the sitting stump and a bush of bright red berries. It was then that her life changed forever.

CHAPTER 16

THE BIG WISH

———

Like her grandmother before her, Button sat awhile on the stump overlooking the creek, eating ripe red berries from the bush that made fruit unlike anything she'd ever tasted. Though she was quite aware that she would probably get in trouble with her grandma for digging up the unicorn horn, she also knew that there was only so much trouble her grandma could get her in without her mom knowing why.

Though she had been tempted to return to the island in the middle of the lake to retrieve her pile of mermaid scales, she ultimately decided that they were safe where they were for the moment. She wanted to see proof of her grandma's other notorious story—the unicorn in the forest.

Giddy with excitement at what she might unearth, she got to work and began digging until her hard work paid off. She found a dirty tin box, hidden in the tangle of roots, and pulled it out. As she dusted it off, she realized it was locked.

Irritated, she sat down on a pile of turned-up earth and began to fiddle with the lock. She tried picking it with various twigs but couldn't seem to get it open.

"You should try the key," a small scratchy voice said behind her.

Button jumped and dropped the box. Wheeling around, she came face to face with a large black crow. Its head was tilted looking at her.

"Did you just—?"

"Yes. I think you'd have better luck with the key, is all," the crow said and hopped up next to her on the log.

"Well, I don't have the key," said Button, completely bewildered.

"You do have the key. It's hidden in the place you hide all things."

"How do you know where I hide things?"

"You're not the only one who steals from the baskets," the crow said, cawing in laughter. "I spent many years collecting those charms. But I won't live forever. Successors must be made or else rituals are lost."

"I mean, it's just a silly belief," said Button. "People would still have babies if they didn't leave baskets on the island."

"Hope is important, no matter how it's delivered."

"Hope," repeated Button. "So, the key to this box is in our pile of trinkets?" She stood up.

"Let me take you," said the crow. "Crawl on my back."

"But you're so small," she argued.

"I am not small," the crow said and stretched out its wings, growing before her eyes to the size of a small pony. "Crawl on my back."

Button was so shocked by this development that she froze for a moment. Was this really happening? She reached out tentatively to touch the crow's back, thick with oversized black feathers shining in the sun. Then, once she had decided it was as real as it could get, she crawled on and wrapped her arms around its neck.

With a great leap, the crow lifted into the air and flew high above the forest. Button held on tight as the bird's wings flapped under her legs. She could see the whole town and marveled at the roofs of the houses, the varying depths of the lake, the people walking about far below her. She wondered how it was that nobody seemed to notice the huge bird flying above.

When they landed, Button slid off the bird's back and caught her breath. Upon looking again, the crow had returned to normal size.

Shrugging this off, she went straight to the hole in the ground and climbed down to find the stash of trinkets and mermaid scales. The crow waited aboveground and called down to her, "When you find it, bring the key up here, and we will open the box together."

Button had other ideas. With the tin box under her arm, she carefully picked through the trinkets until she found a dainty little key attached to a necklace chain. She set down the tin on top of the pile of scattered mermaid scales and fitted the key inside the lock. She was desperate to know everything.

When she turned the key and opened the box, she found two more mermaid scales and a silver, spiraled unicorn horn. But before she could take in her discoveries, the scales inside and outside of the box began to shine, and the unicorn horn began to shake. Reflexively, she grabbed the horn. There was a sudden burst of white light, and she fell onto the cave floor, unconscious.

The distressed cawing of a crow.
A telepathic unicorn.
A mermaid with breasts that sagged and swayed in
    the water.
The locket her grandmother wore.
Bright light. White bright light.
Sisters who loved and hated.

Cousins who turned away from each other.
Mothers and daughters.
Rain on the mountains.
Bits of glittery souls.
Two boys hauling water buckets.
A lake town drying up.
The distressed cawing of a crow.

* * *

When Button finally came to, she blinked and rubbed her eyes. Everything was scattered about the cave floor. Hastily, she got up, scooped the unicorn horn and all the mermaid scales into the tin box, locked it, and put the key necklace around her neck and under her shirt.

She climbed up the ladder and looked around. The crow was gone. She walked toward the edge of the island that faced home and sighed. She'd have to swim back to shore.

She found the house empty when she arrived home, changed into fresh clothes, hung her wet clothes on the line outside, then laid down in the living room with her tin tucked under her arm. The last thing she saw before falling asleep was the bright swirl of colors she'd painted on the floor.

* * *

It wasn't until her parents came home that Button began to wonder what had truly happened to her in the cave on the island when she'd opened the box. She woke up to the smell of dinner wafting from the kitchen and a blanket draped over her.

"Dinner's ready," her mom called from the kitchen.

Button wrapped the blanket around her shoulders and stood up. First, the box. She went down the hallway to her room and tucked it under her pillow, then came back out and sat at the table next to her dad who was reading as he waited.

"How many times have I told you not to read at the table?" Anne asked. Frank sighed.

"You've told him exactly twice every week for the past six months, but he has no intention of stopping," Button recounted in a bored voice, then her eyes grew wide at the words that fell out of her mouth.

They both looked at her, then looked at each other.

"Button, watch your mouth," her mother said.

"Sorry," she said. How had she come up with the answer to that so fast? She brushed it off, and Anne brought the food to the table. They served themselves quietly.

"I heard in town today that Nicole's sons might be starting work on the old bridge," Anne said offhandedly. Though generally a quiet woman in town, she liked to discuss its goings-on at home with her family.

"They are," Button replied simply before her dad could get in a word. "They aren't happy about it, though, and if they aren't supervised, Ernest will do a sloppy job on the railing. The first time it's bumped, it will fall."

"Excuse me?" her dad asked.

"Sorry," she said. "Mouth. Watching it." She began to cut at her chicken with her knife and fork as she tried to grapple with the extraordinary lack of control she had over her tongue.

"How could you possibly know if they aren't happy about getting that job?" Anne asked.

"I just know," said Button. But she didn't know why she'd said what she did, or what had compelled her, or where the information was even coming from. She put her hand on her forehead to check her temperature.

Anne clocked this. "Are you feeling okay?"

"Yeah," said Button. "I'm not going to get sick for at least the next year."

"Oh, I get it," Frank said. "You're predicting things. Is that what the game is?"

Anne and Frank shared little knowing smiles. This was obviously just another silly thing their daughter had come up with to entertain herself and annoy them.

"What do you want to know?" Button said, but her mouth felt foreign, and her eyelids felt heavy. She tried to focus on eating, but she could feel her parents' eyes on her.

"I want to know the next time that we'll see your cousins again," Anne said.

"Within the next month, but if we don't ask for a family dinner when we see them next, there won't be any more."

"Okay, we'll have to remember to ask. Will we become grandparents someday?" Frank asked.

"Yes, but you'll never know the baby."

"Bella Button!" Anne snapped. "That's not funny. I don't care if you're joking. That's not funny."

Button's eyes bubbled up with tears. She knew it wasn't funny. She didn't understand what was happening to her.

"Just send me to my room, please," she said quietly.

"I will not. You will sit here and eat dinner with us and keep your mean jokes to yourself. Do you understand me?"

Button nodded. As her parents swapped faces of confusion at their daughter's behavior, she looked out the window. The crow was sitting on the sill, looking at her. When she saw it, it cawed.

"Excuse me," Button said hastily and ran out the front door before her parents could stop her. The crow met her on the porch.

"You opened the box," it said in the same small scratchy voice from earlier. "And you took on too much power."

"What does that mean? What's going on?"

"You are a Seer. You got your wish and you now have a gift."

"I didn't make a wish."

"You did. You wanted to know everything. Look at the burned mermaid scales in your box. Though eventually, they may regain some of their power, they are weak now. Be wise with this wish and remember to look for the hope somewhere beyond the truth." The crow cawed and then took off into the night sky.

Button walked back inside and sat down at the dinner table.

"What were you doing?" Anne asked. "You're acting really strange, Button."

"Sorry." Button began to cut apart her chicken again. "It turns out that I accidentally became a medium today."

Her parents rolled their eyes at her. Button did her best to finish eating quickly, then headed straight to bed.

She lay awake thinking of the possibilities and the downfalls that came with knowing everything. She hadn't *meant* to wish for this, and she didn't know whether to feel scared or elated. On one hand, she didn't know how much exercise she could control over the truth gushing out of her mouth; she thought about the way she'd hurt her parents at dinner. But then again, if she really *did* know everything, she might be able to help the people around her.

The next day, Button went to see her Grandma Rose. When she arrived, Rose was sitting on the back porch of the little house gazing out into the forest and whittling a stick absentmindedly.

"Hey, Grandma," Button said as she sat down on the bench beside her.

"Heard you had some razzle-dazzle berries," Rose said casually and glanced at her granddaughter, brow furrowed.

"How did you know?" Button asked.

"I didn't." Rose smiled. "But now I do."

Button grumbled. "Okay, okay, fine. I went and ate the berries and dug up your box and met this weird crow and found the key and a million things happened. And it turns out that I'm a Seer now."

Rose raised her eyebrows at this. "Really? Do tell."

Button explained what had happened all the way through accidentally making predictions at the dinner table with her family then looked up at Rose, expecting to get in trouble.

"Hmm," Rose said. "And the mermaid scales are really burned?"

"Yeah," Button said. "They look like they could crumble into ash at any minute." She pulled out the tin box from her dress pocket and opened it to show Rose. But when she opened it, she was startled to see that all the mermaid scales—every single one—had gained a little color back. Faint silver and blue hues filled the box and glinted off the inside walls of the tin.

"They don't look burned to me," Rose said.

Button looked at the mermaid scales incredulously. She wished she could show Rose what they looked like before.

As soon as the thought crossed her mind, though, the unicorn horn began shaking, and the scales began to glow red as if they were on fire. Button grabbed the unicorn horn in an attempt to keep it still. Once it stopped, she put it back in the box with the scales, only to find the scales looking burnt as they had the day before.

"Look." She showed Rose. "I wished that they looked burnt, and now they are."

Rose raised her eyebrows at this. Button was too feisty to have so much power. Then again, Rose hadn't felt prepared for leadership at that age either, but she'd done okay.

"So that begs the question: what did you wish when you first opened the box?"

"I just wanted to know what was in the box," Button shrugged. "I was thinking what I'm always thinking—that I want to know everything."

"And now you can See," said Rose flatly. "You wished on the whole pile of them, all at once, that you could know everything."

Rose looked like a wilting flower as she sat slumped over on the bench with her face in her hands, thinking.

"Not to jump the gun or anything," Button ventured, "but I thought it would be cool to set up a fortune-telling stand by the lake somewhere. I spent all night thinking about how the crow kept emphasizing that people need hope. I think maybe I could actually do some good with this kind of power. I mean, I'll need practice learning how to be less blunt, but maybe there are things I can prevent or at least help people prepare for." Button looked at her grandma earnestly.

Rose was suddenly hit with the memory of when she was young and full of life, like her granddaughter. Button might be a little wild, and her good intentions often trailed behind her actions in the form of apologies, but still. Her eyes were bright, and her belief in the experience with the crow reminded Rose of how she'd felt with the unicorn. It was hard to believe in magic alone, but now she could share it with Button.

"I think with some practice, that would be a wonderful idea," Rose said. "You can start rehearsing with me."

Button's fortune-telling became an overnight hit. Just as the crow had said, the people of Zophren mainly came for hope. Though there were a few bumpy firsts in which Button predicted an early death and a fight over the biggest fish at the market, she quickly learned to add in bits of advice to her answers. Even if she told people something negative, if they felt like they had a choice in dealing with it, they walked away happy.

One day, though, her cousin Ernest came to visit. She didn't think anything of it. Their relationship wasn't a strong one so when they did see each other, it was friendly and cordial, but nothing more.

"Will my girlfriend say yes when I ask her to marry me?" he asked, putting a coin in the jar and grinning like he already knew the answer.

"No," Button said immediately, "but this is a good thing. She hasn't been faithful."

His face drained. "What?"

"You heard me," Button said. "She's been cheating on you."

"How dare you!" he cried. Button shrank behind the counter of her stand. She'd never seen him yell before. He slammed his fist on the table and walked off in a huff.

When Nicole, his mother, heard of the prediction Button had made that morning, she stomped straight past the fortune-telling stand to Anne's house where she proceeded to yell at Anne about the fortune-telling business ruining lives and tarnishing the good family name. But as Nicole was ripping into her cousin Anne about the fiasco, Ernest and his girlfriend also started yelling at each other on the bridge in town. There wasn't a soul in Zophren who couldn't hear at least one of the two fights.

Button shut down her fortune-telling stand and took her coin jar home. She could hear the fighting between her mom and her aunt from outside the house. She tried to walk past them quietly to hide in her room, but her Aunt Nicole immediately saw her and began digging in.

"You think it's funny to break up a relationship? You broke your cousin's heart, Bella," she snapped. "And for what? Why would you do such a thing?"

Button didn't know what to say but was caught by surprise when her mom cut in for her.

"I've been trying to tell you, Nicole, Bella is a real Seer. She wouldn't lie about something like this. She would never say anything hurtful if it wasn't true. Like it or not, Ernest's girlfriend must have been cheating on him. Wouldn't you rather know now? What if he'd married her?" Anne's chest was puffed out.

Button had never been defended by her mother like this in her life and was almost beginning to enjoy it when Ernest showed up.

His face was tear-streaked and red as he came through the door. Immediately, he shot Button a dirty look and muttered to his mom that they really ought to go home now.

"What are you talking about, Ernest? I'm not done asking your cousin why she thought it was okay to ruin your proposal."

"She just told the truth, Mom," he said quietly.

Nicole, taken aback at this, gaped at him. "It's true?"

"Oh, you'll believe your son, but not your cousin," Anne huffed. "I told you it was true. Now get out!" She shooed Nicole and Ernest toward the door.

"And you!" Anne wheeled around toward Button once they'd left. "What were you *thinking* telling your idiot cousin the actual truth?"

"I thought he would be better off knowing," Button said sadly. "But I didn't look further than that, and I should have. Now we'll never see Aunt Nicole or any of them again."

Anne frowned at this. "We won't?"

"No," said Button. "She's going to convince the town that I'm a witch."

"She can't," said Anne, horrified.

"She will. I need to be out of town within two days."

***

Rose came to the fortune-telling stand the next day. Button was doing her best to sell as many fortunes as possible in preparation for having to leave town. The whispers had already begun.

"For you, my dear," Rose said and handed over the golden locket she'd worn her whole life. "I can feel the end coming. Can you tell me if I'm right?"

Button took one look at her grandmother and knew. Quietly, she said, "It will hurt, but it won't take long. This afternoon." Almost immediately, tears began to form in her eyes.

Rose dropped a considerable amount of money into the coin jar as Button tried to swallow the sobs coming up her throat. She didn't like being asked to look at her grandma's death, especially when Rose was the only person in the world who knew about magic the way she did.

"I'll miss you, my love. Carry on our stories."

"I will." A hot tear fell down Button's cheek. "I have something else to tell you. I told Ernest that his girlfriend was cheating on him and now Nicole is going to tell the town I'm a witch. I have to leave by tomorrow or risk—"

"Will everything be okay once you leave?" Rose asked sharply. Button nodded. "Then go. Have some adventures for me, okay? Give your parents a hug, then off you go to explore the world." She kissed Button's forehead. "Oh, and can you give this to Michael and Ernest on your way out?" She handed Button an envelope.

"What is it?"

"A letter telling them where to find the clean water. You told me last week the drought will come in five years."

Button nodded and put the envelope in her pocket, gave Rose one last hug, and watched her walk home for the last time. Unable to stand it, she ran home to tell her mom. But by the time she and Anne made it to the big house, Rose was already gone.

CHAPTER 17

BUTTON SEES THE SEA

———

After exchanging tearful goodbyes with her parents and assuring them that things would settle once she was gone, Button packed up the tin of magic, her money, some clothes, then set off on her adventure in the evening after dinner. There was no reason to wait until morning. She left Rose's letter tucked in her cousins' mailbox, then walked with her head down on her way out of town toward Nia.

She didn't want to think about the mess she'd left behind in Zophren for her parents to deal with. But Button knew that without her there to be used as a scapegoat, Nicole would eventually forget about her grudge and things would go back to normal. Or as normal as they could be without herself or Rose there.

After several hours of walking, she sat down on the side of the road to rest for the night. A traveler on horseback found her sometime after dark and mistook her for dead. But as he began to rifle through her pockets, she woke up and screamed. He jumped back, yelling in alarm.

"Are you trying to rob me?" she shouted, indignant.

"I thought you were dead!"

"Well, I'm not!"

"Obviously," he laughed. "What are you doing sleeping on the side of the road?"

Maybe it was the late hour, but his laugh sounded young. They might have been close in age. And though she couldn't see him too clearly in the dark, she could make out a lean, muscled silhouette.

"Well, I wasn't trying to lure thieves," Button responded.

"Sorry," he apologized. "If it makes you feel better, I always bury the dead bodies I find after I rob them."

"Really?"

"No, actually I eat them. Yes," he said teasingly. "But maybe I can offer you a ride now that I know I don't have to bury you?"

"Oh, sure," Button snorted. "I'm just dying to get on a horse with you and lose all my money the minute I nod off."

"It doesn't have to be like that," he purred and came closer to her. "I would be happier to have company than a few extra coins in my purse."

Button blushed in the dark. "Where are you headed? I'm a fortune-teller, and I need a new crowd to impress. That means I'll know if you steal from me."

"I'm on my way to Nia," he told her. "Maybe you can start with impressing *me*. If you tell me what time we'll make it there, I'll give you a ride."

"Sure, I'd appreciate that," she said, carefully tucking her money as far down in her pockets as she could and looking into the future. Startled, she saw herself marrying this man. She did her best to ignore that particular vision and answered his question.

"We'll make it to Nia as the sun begins to rise, but since you live farther up the mountain, we'll get to your place after it's already risen."

"Oh? You want to go to my place?" he asked.

She burst out laughing. "Well, thanks. I thought you'd never ask!"

"You're a wild one," he said, impressed. "Come on, then."

She got on his horse with him, and they rode the rest of the night to Nia. She fell asleep with her head on his back. She knew he wouldn't steal from her.

It turned out that the young man was named Charlie, and when he wasn't selling strange herbs, medicines, or tonics on the sides of the roads—or just plain stealing—he was very able with his hands and worked as a carpenter. Though what he really wanted was to own a bar.

He took her to his small house up the side of the mountain. It had two rooms and was empty inside except for a large pile of blankets in the corner and cups and pans in the kitchen. He carried Button in and made a bed for her on the floor. When they woke up in the morning, they talked and kissed until they decided that they were absolutely, definitely in love. Button helped this along by teasing in some of the things she saw them doing together in the future, but she didn't dare look much farther than a month ahead. Her new life away from Zophren was supposed to be an adventure, but how adventurous could it be if she kept looking ahead?

She wrote to her parents after about a week, once she'd had the time to help Charlie make his house a little more livable. She didn't say much, just that she'd made it to Nia and was busy trying to adjust to her new life.

After she got settled into Charlie's house, Button set up her fortune-telling stand out in the streets of Nia and found that the people wanted essentially the same as the people of Zophren: hope. She was busy answering questions a couple of months after she'd set up shop when a letter came by messenger to the town square.

"Letter for Bella Button?" the messenger called.

She immediately claimed the letter and opened it.

Bella Button,

Thank you for sending word. We hope you are doing well. Things have settled down here in Zophren, just as you said they would. Nicole got half the town to believe you were a witch before the truth finally came out. Though she has mostly let it go and has returned to being civil toward us, I don't know if we'll ever be able to truly forgive her. Your cousin Michael asked us to tell you 'thank you' for delivering your Grandma Rose's letter to him. He told us you had given him a fortune before you left that will help the town if the lake does dry up. We miss you very much and hope you haven't gotten yourself into trouble.

Love,
Mom and Dad

Button sighed. She missed them, but it wasn't worth Aunt Nicole's rage to go back. It wouldn't be the same without her Grandma Rose, and anyway, she could see all kinds of adventurous possibilities with Charlie. As she folded up the letter and put it in her pocket, Charlie came running up to her.

"Button, I've got big news!" He pulled her close. "I've just received word that a ship to a new world goes out in a few months, out of Schi, and they're hiring for crew starting tomorrow. If you go over as crew, you don't have to pay for yourself or your wife."

"Do you have experience on boats?"

"Nope," said Charlie cheerfully, "but I'm happy to learn on the job. And I'm an excellent liar."

She laughed. "And what's this about wives? We're not married. Don't tell me you've already got a wife."

He grinned and pulled a piece of paper out of his pocket. "We can be married today, if you still want to."

She did. Not caring to see what their future as husband and wife might hold, she kissed him in front of the courthouse witness and daydreamed about what it might be like to arrive in a brand-new world.

Right before going to bed, Button stayed up to pen a letter to her parents. In it, she simply wrote that she was glad to hear that bygones had become bygones, but that she was now married and would be moving across the ocean soon. She promised to send an address once they found a place to live. In the meantime, if they wanted, they could come see her and her husband off in Schi in a couple of months. She knew that they would read this letter with a mix of exasperation, sadness, and relief when they got it. But she also knew that they wouldn't come see her and Charlie off. Fleetingly, she thought about the night she became a Seer and how she accidentally told her parents that they would never know their grandchild, but she shoved this thought away as soon as it arrived. She was beginning to grow tired of knowing everything. With this thought in mind, she reached for her tin full of magic but, after touching the lid, decided against it and went to bed.

* * *

When Button awoke in the early dark of the next morning, she felt queasy and didn't eat much breakfast. She thought she felt a little ill because she missed her parents.

As she and Charlie made their way to Schi, Button looked up at the moon and realized immediately why she was sick. The full moon was already several days gone.

"Charlie," she said as they left town. "I have to tell you something."

"What is it? Are you okay?"

"I think I'm pregnant."

Charlie pulled the horse up and stopped. She looked worried. Not knowing what to say, he went with humor.

"Use your Seer skills. Is it going to be a boy or a girl?"

"It's going to be a..." Button stopped short. "I don't know." Her face wrinkled in confusion. "Why don't I know?"

Charlie didn't know what to say. "Maybe that's just one thing in life nobody can predict."

"No," she said. "I've done it before for others. That's really strange." She wondered if simply by touching the tin the night before, she'd accidentally made another wish.

Charlie kissed her. "That's alright. I like surprises."

"You do?" she asked uncertainly. "Ask me something else."

"Of course." He grinned. "How about: will our baby grow up in the new world?"

"Yes," she answered, puzzled at the quickness with which the answer came.

"Good," he said.

* * *

Five months later, Button's belly had grown immensely, and they boarded the ship to cross the ocean. It was crowded, and they shared tight quarters with three other couples.

Charlie took to the work like an old hand, but he hardly saw Button at all. She almost immediately got seasick and only ventured out of her bunk for meals and bathroom breaks. The ship reeked of unwashed people, which also contributed to her queasiness.

It wasn't an easy journey. Though they'd left Schi on a warm and windy day, that was about the last time the weather cooperated. They went from dead in the water on still days to crashing through angry seas when storms hit.

Finally, in the eleventh week of back-and-forth, they hit a good stride of wind and finally made quick paces toward the promised land. Button was in her eighth month by this time. The captain was optimistic that day and so was Charlie when he came back to the bunk, exhausted from a hard day's work.

"We're almost there," he whispered to Button as he crawled into bed next to her.

"Mmm, I hope so," she groaned.

"When we get close, I want you to come on deck with me so we can see everything," he said, rubbing her belly. "It will be just in time for you to give birth. We'll find a nice doctor and a house, and…"

"Charlie…" she gasped.

"What? I think we can find a house, no problem. With your fortune-telling money, and my—"

"No, Charlie, no!" Button began writhing next to him. "The baby!" She started crying.

"What? What's wrong?"

He felt a warm spot creep toward him on the mattress. "Oh, no," he murmured.

"It's time, I can't—" she sobbed.

"You can," he said, panic rising in his voice. "It's okay. I'll go get somebody, don't move." He jumped out of the bunk.

"Keep an eye on her," he said to the others in the room, then ran out the door into the hallway yelling for a doctor.

One of the women stood up and spoke gently to Button to try and soothe her, but she was quickly becoming inconsolable. "Get Charlie," she cried in between heaves of pain.

Something was wrong, she could tell. Incomprehensible futures were flashing rapidly in her mind as pain came crashing in increasingly violent crescendos.

The cawing of a crow.
A puddle of bright blood.
A girl named Rosie.
The ocean floor.
A bar and a baby.
Grandma Rose.
The stories.
The locket.
A black crow's dead body.

Charlie rushed back without a doctor when he heard her screams get louder. By this time, Button was on all fours on the bunk in full-bodied contractions, sobbing.

"Charlie," she whispered between gasps for air. "I can See again. Name her Rosie after my grandma."

"A girl?"

"Tell her the stories I told you. All of them."

"The unicorn? The island? The—!"

"Yes, tell her the stories. Name her Rosie. Give her my necklace, my grandma's necklace."

"You're not going to die," he assured her.

"Write my parents a letter," she sobbed.

Charlie pulled the baby out amid Button's cries. Once delivered, he handed her over to the woman closest to him, who wrapped her in bedsheets.

Button continued to sob and contract until a placenta slid out. Charlie cut the cord with his knife as she rolled over to lay on her back. The blood soaked through the mattress and dripped on the floor. The baby began to cry.

Charlie took a deep breath and said proudly, "You did it. Look at our baby." He reached over to take the baby from the woman's arms and put her on Button's chest, but just as he was doing so, Button violently seized.

Charlie quickly handed the baby back to the woman, then froze in panic. Blood gushed out of Button in uncontrollable waves; her eyes squeezed shut. She twisted around, screaming and gasping in pain. Charlie tried to stop the bleeding with all the sheets he could get his hands on but couldn't apply the pressure evenly as her whole body jolted around the bed violently.

"Button! You've got to stay still, it's going to be okay," Charlie shouted as he tried to hold her still. Button gasped for breath, eyes still closed but leaking streams of tears. Charlie cried and crawled on top of her to keep her still, using his knees to keep the wad of sheets in place to soak up the blood. He held her shoulders down and put his head on her chest.

"You can't," he sobbed. "Just breathe, just breathe. You can't leave me."

The seizure was slowly losing steam, and her body quieted to jerky twitches instead of violent jolts. But her breathing became labored, and her stomach was sucking itself in with such force that, even with the remaining bubble of pregnancy left, it caved in like a bowl as she choked.

"Don't leave me, don't leave me, please. Just breathe."

Charlie put his hand on one of her cheeks, and she opened her eyes to meet his one last time before her body finally went limp, and her last breath left her. He sat frozen above her for a moment before gently closing her eyelids. Then he reached out silently for his baby. Charlie carefully placed Rosie on her mother's chest, and they both cried themselves to sleep.

They were three days from shore.

Charlie carried his daughter, Rosie, wrapped in a bedsheet, off the boat when they arrived. Carefully tucked under that bedsheet was the golden locket around Rosie's neck and a wad of cash her dad, in his anxiety of being a single parent, pickpocketed on the way out.

Rosie, the first namesake of Rose's bloodline, had made it to a brand-new world with just a golden locket and the stories her dad would spend years telling her of her ancestors.

CHAPTER 18

THE FIRST NAMESAKE

———

Though Charlie didn't find a house as quickly as he'd planned, he did manage to make plenty of friends who were more than happy to let him stay with them as he and Rosie rolled through towns. It turned out his knack for petty theft also came in handy between proper jobs. As she grew, Rosie picked up on this skill quickly. She became a master at shoving candy up the sleeves of her coat the minute she was old enough to walk and talk.

By the time Rosie was about eight, they'd settled down in a small town where Charlie worked both as a handyman and fur trader. Rosie went to the one-room school sometimes, but mostly she picked up odd jobs to make money. They spent a few years sleeping in a farmer's barn as a deal to work the harvest in the summer. But eventually, between the two of them, Charlie and Rosie had enough money to buy a bar.

They opened the bar together when Rosie was fifteen years old, right next to a frequently visited trading post. That's when they both felt they'd finally clawed their way out of the abject poverty they'd slummed around in for all of Rosie's childhood.

But for as poor as they were, they weren't miserable at all. Charlie looked at life as an adventure and, while Rosie was sometimes put in a little bit of danger, she loved it. Charlie kept his promise to her mother, Button, and did his best to tell the stories that she'd told him before she died. Having never known her mom, Rosie asked for the stories often—especially the one about the crow. Her mom seemed like the kind of person who pushed boundaries. Rosie admired that.

She wore her mom's necklace at all times; it was the only proof that she'd had a mother. Though she liked to daydream about her mom's Grandma Rose, the woman she was named after, it wasn't the mystical stories of unicorns, crows, or mermaids that she focused on. Instead, she focused on understanding how it must have felt for Rose to have been so alone, yet something so special.

* * *

A couple of years went by before Rosie, with all her charm as a bartender, landed a boyfriend in one of the regulars, a young man with something to prove. His name was Andrew, but he went by Drew. Though her father wasn't fond of Drew—Charlie could recall a few times he'd had to send him home for being too drunk and rowdy—he was at least satisfied that, if nothing else, he could keep a close eye on him, maybe even put him to work.

Rosie and Drew were soon married and Charlie, as a wedding gift, put the ownership of the bar in both their names.

For a few years, things ran smoothly. Rosie was a natural leader and ran the bar with style. Charlie was proud to have raised such an ambitious daughter and was giddy with excitement when, a few months after the wedding, Rosie announced that she was pregnant. Her marriage to Drew became something like a business deal, and this worked for them. Drew took on stocking and purchasing all the things they sold, alcohol and otherwise.

But Rosie's marriage soon faced trouble.

"I think Drew is taking a little from the top of our whiskey stock," Charlie told Rosie late one evening when the bar was full, and Drew was drinking across the room.

"Daddy!" Rosie reprimanded. "You can't just go around accusing him of things."

Charlie put his hands up. "It's your bar, baby. I just wanted to make sure you knew."

Rosie scoffed and put it out of her mind. But when she reviewed the inventory later that night, she found that her dad was right.

Rosie confronted Drew about it the next morning once he'd sobered up and had his coffee. Vehemently, he denied things until Rosie showed him the records. Then his argument turned.

"It's *our bar*," he said. "We pay for that whiskey so why can't I keep a little for us?"

"For you," she said. "I don't drink whiskey."

"So why not?"

"We lose money that way, and there's more than enough that we already set aside for us to drink. You're being greedy."

"That's shit. It's our bar, and I'll take what I deserve."

The argument got worse the longer they went back and forth until, finally, Rosie stormed out and went straight to her dad.

"You were right," she cried to him. "What do I do?"

Charlie frowned. "You need to make him get another job. I'll take care of the rest."

"Another job? Where?"

"He worked at the mill before. Have him ask the boss if they'll take him back. Tell him he needs to make more money so you can afford more whiskey."

"Yeah. If we just had more whiskey…" Rosie trailed off. "What are you going to do?"

Charlie grinned. "I'm going to get him drunk and have him sign the papers that will take away his ownership of the bar."

"What? That will just make things worse. Forget it," Rosie said.

Charlie shrugged. "Okay, if you don't want me to, I won't. But I mean it when I say that Drew can't be trusted with the responsibility of helping you run that bar, and this won't be the last time he costs you. Besides, if I get him drunk enough, he'll be none the wiser."

"If he just gets his job at the mill back, everything will be fine," Rosie decided with finality.

After Rosie made her point, Drew went back to the mill, and Rosie set aside more whiskey to satiate him. The bar flourished, and within the year, Rosie gave birth to a beautiful daughter who she named Mary.

Rosie kept busy managing the bar. Charlie was the one who watched over Mary during the afternoons until Drew came home from the mill to take over while Rosie worked late into the nights. Though Drew was drinking more whiskey than before, he seemed happy with the arrangement and did his best to be the kind of father that was around—even if he was drunk for most of it.

A few years passed this way, and Mary grew up to be a quiet but happy addition to the family. She loved following her Grandpa Charlie around, and Rosie encouraged her to ask about the stories of her grandmother and the rest of their ancestors. But when she did, Charlie told Mary that they were her mom's stories to pass down, not his.

Though Rosie was often busy during afternoons and nights, her favorite time soon became the mornings that she and Mary got to spend together. These were when they could tell secrets, just the two of them, and Rosie could tell Mary what a magical family history they both had. Though she loved her husband, Drew, Rosie had resigned herself to the kind of man he was. But Rosie felt like she and her daughter had something truly special.

Once Mary was old enough for school, her dad stopped spending as many evenings at home with her. She was old enough, he figured, to be at the house by herself or come along with him to the bar where he began spending more nights again.

Rosie wasn't amused with this logic but gracefully figured out how to use Mary's help around the bar or send her into the kitchen to read or do her homework. But as Drew became more accustomed to drinking the way he had in the early years of their marriage, Rosie's love for him began to crumble. His drinking eventually crossed the line. Rosie began hiding the bruises with long-sleeved shirts.

Mary knew what was happening and stayed close to her mom when they were all at home together. Though Rosie did her best to pretend that nothing was wrong, one night when Mary was thirteen changed everything.

Drew had run through the whiskey and was in the middle of stealing rum when Rosie and Mary caught him. They had come in to prep the bar for opening, and two of the regulars were waiting outside to be let in. To nobody's surprise, Drew was already quite drunk.

"Dad!" Mary reprimanded him when they saw him on the floor rummaging through the cabinet.

"Leave me alone," he huffed.

"Get out of that cabinet," Rosie said and went to pull him up by his armpits. But he wasn't drunk enough to drag.

That day, he was drunk enough to fight. The minute Rosie attempted to drag him away from the liquor cabinet, he turned around and swung right at her face. Rosie was no stranger to this and took the punch before attempting to hit him back. He caught her wrist and twisted 'til it cracked. Though Mary had seen the bruises and cuts, this was the first time she'd seen the action firsthand.

"Stop it!" Mary cried and ran to intervene. But Drew threw a bottle of tequila at her, and it shattered on the floor. Screaming, she ran out of the front door to go find her grandpa or the police or somebody, and the two regulars who were waiting outside came into a bar that had begun to turn bloody. Drew was slashing Rosie with shards of glass from the broken tequila bottle; she attempted to break free of his hold to dash out the front door after her daughter.

"Hey, man! Leave her be!" one of the regulars shouted. They both came over to break up the fight, but by the time they'd pulled him off her, the damage was done. Glass cuts, a black eye, a broken wrist, and a daughter who would never trust her father again.

Drew didn't know it at the time, but Mary ran to her Grandpa Charlie to tell him what happened. Though Charlie immediately wanted to kill Drew, Mary insisted that they just needed to figure out how to hide the alcohol from him. Charlie nodded. He carried out the plan he'd offered to carry out years ago to Mary's mother. He was going to take Drew's property rights away, and with them, the keys to the bar.

Only half of the plan worked; though Drew drunkenly signed away all his rights, he simply stole Rosie's keys to the bar after assuming he'd lost his and snuck in while she was asleep at home when he needed to raid the liquor stock. Once, though, he got blackout drunk and tried to give away free bottles to everyone. When the cops came to arrest him, he tried to tell them that the bar and its contents were his property. They told him it wasn't, and he spent the night in jail. Rosie and Mary worried that when he got out, he would be livid, but it turned out that he was so drunk he thought that he had been jailed for fighting or being too drunk in public.

One day, when Mary was fifteen and working part-time as a seamstress down the street, her father dug through the closet at home trying to find the extra wine Rosie always set aside for parties. His pile of whiskey had dried up, and so had the stock at the bar. But as he went through the closet, he found the paperwork that he'd signed so many years ago that took away his right to the bar.

His scream of rage was heard all down the street, and when Mary heard gunshots ring out, she dropped what she was doing and ran to her house as fast as she could.

When she got there, her Grandpa Charlie was already beating down the door. Loud bangs and screams came from inside. It sounded as though furniture was being thrown. Then another gunshot. More screaming ensued.

"Go back to work, Mary," Charlie said when he saw her.

"No!" cried Mary. "My mama's in there!"

But by the time Charlie broke down the door, the house had fallen silent. Drew lay dead on the middle of the floor in a pool of blood, and Rosie was trying to pull herself up onto one of the kitchen chairs. She was bleeding, too, from her stomach.

"What happened?" Charlie rushed in to help his daughter. Mary stood in the doorway in shock.

"He found out," Rosie gasped. "About the rights to the bar. He was out of whiskey."

"Are you hurt bad? Let me see," Charlie said and raised her dress to see her stomach, but as he did, she moaned in pain and fell to her knees. He helped her sit on the floor in between his legs, propping her torso against his and leaned forward gently to look at the stab wounds in her stomach: deep, twisted things given to her by the largest kitchen knife Drew could find.

Her eyes rolled back from the pain, and Charlie gently pulled her close and began to sob. "It's okay, baby girl. I got you. I'm right here, Rosie."

He motioned to Mary to come over, and she did, holding tight her mother's hand and brushing the hair out of her face as her mom winced and struggled to breathe.

"Here," she said to Mary and reached for her necklace. Charlie helped her take it off.

"This is yours now. Be strong," she gasped, and with a rattling breath, she was gone.

CHAPTER 19

DEMONS AND THE REBEL GIRL

———

Mary, in her grief, took it upon herself to document in writing all of the stories her mom had told her. She spent ten years living with her grandfather, Charlie, who once again owned the bar. She spent those years writing and working as a seamstress. At her insistence, Charlie told her all he could about her father, Drew, making her wary of men altogether. Despite this, she still fell in love with a calm farmer, Judd, and got married. When Charlie offered to help them buy a house together, Mary declined.

"I don't want his name on anything, Grandpa," she told him, and he understood.

Once Mary had saved up enough money, she bought them a small house in town under her name. Though they primarily lived in the house on his farmland, it made Mary feel better owning her own property, and they stayed there often on the weekends when they came to town for shopping and to visit Charlie.

They had a son and daughter together: Garrett and Joanna. Garrett was almost an exact replica of his dad; he took to farming like an old hand, had an even temperament, and mostly kept to himself. Joanna, on the other hand, was nothing Mary expected her to be.

Mary shared—almost desperately—the stories her mom, Rosie, had passed down to her. The first Rose, the unicorn, the mermaid, the crow, the ship to the new world, and all the rest. But Joanna wasn't interested in "those fairytales," and told Mary as much.

Mary did her best to warn her of men, especially men who drank or behaved recklessly with property because of what had happened with her own parents. But Joanna wasn't interested in listening to her mother's paranoid warnings about this, either.

Joanna instead became part of one of the new churches in town, a church that owned a tent just down the street from their townhouse. Mary and Judd, however, weren't sure it could even be called a church. The one service they attended—just to placate their daughter—didn't mention God or include piano hymns; they had a rock band and explained that anyone could be taken over by demons. It was the congregation's responsibility to bring people they thought had been afflicted to be healed. Joanna was one of the prayer girls who laid hands on people to free them of these demons. It made Mary think of witch hunts and exorcisms, and she wondered what her Grandma Button's fate might have been if she'd stayed in Zophren.

Though mother and daughter didn't understand each other when it came to spiritual awakenings and men, their relationship took a turn when Joanna brought Fred home. Fred was one of the preachers from Joanna's church and was ready to ask for Mary and Judd's permission to marry their daughter.

"Mama, I really love him," Joanna said to Mary. "I know you don't approve of our church, but he is everything I've ever wanted. He can take good care of me."

"I know, baby, but I want you to be able to take care of yourself," Mary said. Though Joanna rolled her eyes, Mary took her outside and dug through the shed in their yard. "You can get married, but first I want you to have some things."

Mary pulled out the typed pages of the stories she had written and handed them to her dubious daughter. "Though I know you think these are silly, I want you to pass them down to your children. Stories are the only way to keep our family history alive."

"I know, Mama. You've told me."

"And I mean it." Mary smiled.

Mary and Judd agreed to gift their townhouse to the happy young couple. Once they told Charlie of their plan, he agreed and bettered the bargain.

"It's time for you to own the bar," he told Mary. "You don't have to run it, I've got a good group of folks hired, but I'm too old to manage it anymore. And then, if it's still important to you, you'll have your own piece of property, still." Mary agreed, Charlie moved in with them, as it was getting harder for him to walk, and they convinced Garrett to help run the bar a couple of times a week.

Joanna and Fred got married, moved into the townhouse, and almost immediately got pregnant. For several months, Joanna stayed locked up in the house on bedrest; her pregnancy proved to be a difficult one from almost the beginning. Fred rose through the ranks of the church during this time and, just before the baby was born, he sold the townhouse, bought the church a shabby brick building downtown, and moved his bedridden wife and himself into the apartment above the new location.

Charlie, Mary, and Judd were not amused by Fred's decision. Together they decided that Mary needed to go stay with Joanna for the birth of the baby to make sure that their daughter was okay and to scope out the living arrangements their granddaughter would be brought into.

When she arrived at the church, Fred greeted her at the door.

"It's not time yet, Mary," he said to her.

"I know," she said, "but it's coming soon, and every girl needs her mother for the birth of her first baby."

"She'll be okay," Fred said, stepping outside and closing the door behind him. "The doctor is on call, and Joanna isn't feeling well. She's asked for no visitors."

"Not even her mother?" Mary asked.

Fred shook his head and shooed a worried Mary away.

Later that week, after returning home from shopping, she found her Grandpa Charlie had passed away peacefully in his sleep. As she sat next to him on the bed crying, Garrett came home to tell her that he'd heard from one of the church members at the bar earlier that Joanna had given birth to a little girl. They had named her Carole.

Mary cried even harder after hearing this news. One family member left the world, another came into it—and she'd missed them both.

* * *

Joanna and Fred did their best to keep their visits with their family limited due to their ideological differences. Mary, Judd, and Garrett believed in God and singing hymns, and they went to church about twice a year to get their fill. But Joanna and Fred were full-time about their beliefs and talented at spotting people inhabited by demons—sometimes even dragging people off the street to take them to the church for a healing. It didn't help matters that Fred had sold the townhouse without consulting the family. But despite her parents' attempts to keep her on the straight and narrow path of freeing herself from demons and learning the signs of inhabited people, Carole began to have other ideas as she grew older. She especially liked to sneak off to see her Uncle Garrett when he was in town at the bar down the street. Sometimes he'd give her a spoonful of rum in her soda and help her with her schoolwork if it was slow.

Mary convinced Joanna and Fred to come to the farm for dinner once a month, and though it wasn't as often as Mary preferred, she loved having that time with her granddaughter. She doted on Carole as much as she could, feeding her homemade ice cream and strawberries from the garden while she passed on her mother's stories. To her delight, Carole listened and asked to touch the locket around her neck more than Joanna ever had.

Mary knew that when the time came, it would be Carole who would inherit the necklace and the typed-up stories. She worried, though, that the stories she had given Joanna might already have been gone. She hadn't thought to make copies.

As a teenager, Carole began to get into trouble, and her parents had different ideas about how to deal with her behavior. Carole began drinking, running around with boys, staying out late, and missing her parents' church services. Though she did well in school, the main issue was that she didn't often show up to class. In her parents' eyes, these were high crimes. The rest of the family let her get away with things, though, which only increased the tension between Joanna and her husband and everyone else. Joanna thought that they simply needed to exercise more control over their daughter, but Fred was ready to send her off to boarding school.

"If we just enforce more rules, she'll figure out that we're not kidding," Joanna argued late one night.

"I think it's far past that," Fred said. "There's nothing more we can do for her. She'll be better off going to a full-time school."

"We don't have the money to send her to a boarding school!"

"We have some leftover from selling the townhouse, and I bet we could convince Garrett to give up his share of that nasty old bar. We could sell it, too!"

"I don't know," Joanna said.

"He doesn't want that bar, he wants to farm," Fred argued and marched out the door and down the street to ask his brother-in-law for permission to sell the bar.

Garrett, who didn't like confrontation, told Fred to let him think about it. That night, he gathered his mom and dad to tell them what Fred had asked of him earlier that day. As they were talking over dinner, somebody knocked on the door.

Mary answered the door and found Carole on their doorstep, a large bag on her back.

"Hey, Carole, what are you doing here?" she asked, looking around for her parents.

"I walked here," Carole said simply. "Can I come in?"

"You walked? We're seven miles outside of town!" Mary exclaimed, but Carole just moved past her and walked into the house, setting her large bag down by the door.

Garrett and Judd said hello as she sat down at the dinner table with them.

"The gang's all here, huh?" she asked as she began piling food onto a plate for herself.

"Were your ears burning, honey? We were talking about what we're going to do with you." Judd nudged her teasingly.

Carole groaned. "What? My parents have gotten to you, too?"

Garrett and Judd gave each other nervous glances, but Mary cut in.

"Your father asked your uncle to sell the bar so they could afford to send you to boarding school," she said to her granddaughter.

"Yeah, that's why I'm running away," Carole said flatly. "I'm here to say goodbye. I don't want to go to boarding school."

"We're not selling the bar," Judd said.

"You're not?"

"No," Judd said firmly. "And you're not running away."

"Well, I'm sure as hell not living with my parents anymore," Carole said. "I'm tired of being told I have demons inside me."

"You can live here with us," Judd said. "We'll talk to your parents. We'll figure it out."

But it turned out the solution wouldn't be that easy. The next day, Joanna and Fred arrived at the farm with a local policeman who outlined child custody laws and escorted Carole home. Mary cried into Judd's arms as they left, and Judd swore that they would get their granddaughter back. Over the next year, he worked diligently to find a loophole in the law that would let them take Carole away from her parents. But the next time they saw her, Carole was seventeen and had arrived to say goodbye.

With Joanna and Fred behind her, she stood on the front porch and knocked on the farmhouse door one final time.

"I'm pregnant," she said, between sobs, when Mary opened the door. "And I'm here to say goodbye."

Mary saw the stern faces of her daughter and her husband and frowned.

"You're sending her away?" she asked, and they nodded.

"She made some bad decisions with a young man in town, and she's not ready to raise a child," Fred answered.

"His name is Jesus!" Carole cried.

Joanna made a disapproving noise in her throat.

"Well," said Mary. "If she's here to say goodbye, I have a few things I need to give her." She guided Carole inside by her shoulder but left Joanna and Fred on the front porch, locking the door.

Mary took Carole into the living room and sat her down.

"Remember those stories I told you as a little girl? Of your family? All the histories?" she asked gently as she began to remove the gold locket around her neck.

"Yes," said Carole. "Were they true?"

"All true." Mary smiled. "And it's time you have this necklace, your great-great-great-great-grandmother Rose's locket."

Carole smiled through a sniffle and lifted her hair as her grandma put it around her neck.

"I gave your mother the stories I typed up of our family history when she married your father," Mary started, but Carole interrupted her.

"I know," she said. "I found them a year or two back. She'd buried them deep in her closet."

"Oh, thank goodness," Mary breathed. "Did you take them?"

"I don't have them with me," Carole said. "They went through my bag to make sure I wasn't taking anything they didn't want me to, but I know where they are. I'll come back for them someday."

"Where are they?" Mary asked.

"They're at the bar. Tell Uncle Garrett that I hid them behind the party wine." Carole touched the necklace around her neck again, then tucked it under her shirt.

"Okay, I'll tell him. When will you be back?"

"I don't know. They're putting me in an adoption home where I'll live until I give birth to the baby. And after that, I'm supposed to go to school and get a job. They said the home would help me with all that. I have to make enough money to make it back on my own." She began to cry and fell into her grandma's arms.

"Okay, honey. Write us letters, okay?"

"Okay, I will."

"We love you so much."

"I love you, too."

But Carole never returned.

CHAPTER 20

THE LOST STORIES

———

Carole wrote letters frequently to her grandma during her stay at the adoption home. The first few were about the home, what it was like. Carole told her she was eating spinach to make sure that the baby would be healthy, that the people there were a different breed of religious than her parents but just as strict, that the rooms were nice, and that she liked walking around the grounds to enjoy the gardens. Toward the middle of her pregnancy, her letters took a strange turn.

I think I was wrong about the people here, she wrote. *They really care about me and my baby. They told me I'm doing a good thing. I got baptized yesterday.*

Mary didn't know if this was a true and deep change on Carole's part or if, like Carole had written earlier, the people there were just a different kind of religious and had somehow worn her down. Either way, soon after, Carole happily reported that she'd picked the perfect parents for her baby and found out at her last doctor's visit that she would have a girl.

I know they'll probably change her name, but until then, I'm going to call her Rose. Just like your mom and the first Rose you told me the stories about, Carole wrote.

Though Mary's heart was warmed by this, she wrote back a gentle reminder to her granddaughter that she should try her best not to get too attached. Though her heart ached to write this advice—because she couldn't fathom how hard it would be on Carole to give up her baby—she also knew it would be better if she prepared her for it.

Mary got one last letter from Carole before the new baby Rose was born. It was incomprehensible rambling, containing all the fears and doubts Carole suddenly had about giving her baby up now that she was nearing the end of her pregnancy and could see Rose's feet when she kicked.

I'm going to miss her, she wrote at the end of her letter. *But I'm going to write her letters upon letters. And when she's old enough, I'll find her. We'll be together again.*

Meanwhile, Joanna and Fred were determined to take the bar out from under Garrett, and without the excuse of selling it to use the money to send Carole to boarding school, they decided to hold church protests in front of the bar. They claimed that bars shouldn't be in town, especially not on Main Street where families and children frequently walked.

Garrett did his best to ignore the ruckus outside as the protests went on. But after months of protests costing the bar sales, Judd advised his son to organize the inventory and paperwork just in case they tried to get the law involved or another sale opportunity apart from Joanna and Fred arose.

"Why do you think they want this bar so bad?" Garrett asked his dad.

"It's obviously about the money," Judd answered. "I wonder if they really would have sent Carole to boarding school had they been able to get it back then."

"Do you think they want to fund a bigger church?" Garrett speculated.

"Maybe. Or maybe they just really don't like a nice glass of wine," Judd chuckled.

It was sometime after Garrett finished organizing the last of the paperwork—stacking it neatly in a box to take home that night—that the protesters rushed the building in an angry, violent mob. Garrett called the police, but by the time they arrived, it was too late. Glass window shards, broken chairs, shattered bottles and their contents all littered the floor but, worst of all, the paperwork had been rifled through in the madness. One folder had been stolen out of the box that Garrett, in his panic to call the police, had left sitting on the bar top.

They had stolen Mary's family histories.

Judd, Mary, and Garrett reported the vandalism and theft to the police and submitted their testimonies. But Mary was near hysterical about what she thought must have been a premeditated crime masterminded by her daughter.

"Can you please focus on the theft of the stories we reported? Your best bet is to search Joanna and Fred's house, the two church leaders we mentioned? The bar is our second income, and we aren't too worried about the repairs right away, but those stories are all I have of my family history," Mary begged the police officer.

"I'll look into it right away. Do you have any idea why your daughter might have wanted to steal those papers?"

Mary began crying. "I don't know. She never liked them, she never cared about them, and when she joined that church, something changed. I don't know."

"We think that Joanna and her husband want to take the bar from us and sell it," Judd explained calmly as he patted his wife on the back. "They previously asked us for owner-ship so they could send their daughter to boarding school, but we said no."

"So how does that tie into the family histories?" the police officer asked.

"Maybe she stole it so she could bargain with us? If we give them the bar, they give us the stories?" Garrett offered.

But despite the police's promises to look into it right away, it was two months before a warrant was issued to search Joanna and Fred's residence for the stories.

The search came up empty. The stories were gone.

Later, after an anonymous tip, all the church's leaders were charged and fined, then required to temporarily shut down the church for an investigation into their finances. Whispers around town suggested money laundering. That didn't matter to Garrett, Judd, or Mary. Once they received repair money, Garrett and Judd began to fix up the bar while Mary pestered the police about the stories until they got so annoyed with her, a police officer escorted her home and suggested that if she'd written them before, maybe she could write them again.

Mary tried her best to write again as best she could remember, but it was like trying to catch dreams just out of reach as they faded with wakefulness. Though Judd and Garrett reassured her that she got the important parts down, she knew it wasn't the same and was devastated that she wouldn't be able to pass them down to Carole once she returned home.

It was a year and a half before Mary received another letter from Carole. This one worried Mary more than the others had. Did Joanna and Fred know what they'd done to their daughter?

Grandma Mary,

> *I'm sorry I haven't written. After Rose was born, I didn't have anywhere to go so I live in a homeless camp community now. I won't lie, I fell into drinking and drugs pretty hard, but I'm trying to stop that stuff. It's hard. I'm sad a lot of the time. I wish I could have kept Rose, but I know I wouldn't have been a good mom. They told me I did the right thing and that God would take care of her. She was so beautiful, I couldn't stop crying. You should have seen her.*
>
> *I'm still in a funk a little bit, if I'm honest. I met this girl a few months ago, and she followed me back to camp and hasn't left. It's nice to have a friend, I guess, but there's something off about her. We sometimes have the same dreams. She's running from the cops or somebody, so we've been laying low.*
>
> *Did you find the stories? I hope so. My mom was so mad when she realized I stole them. She thinks all our ancestors were cursed with demons, and that those stories should be burned. I wish I could give you an address to write me back, but I'm kind of undercover right now. I promise I'll send an address when I have one.*

> *Love,*
> *Carole*

Mary showed the letter to Judd, and they decided to pay Joanna and Fred a visit. Judd thought the best way to wiggle into casual conversation about Carole would be to come with a big prize. By this time, Garrett had fixed up the bar so well it looked better than it did before the mob. He was ready to sell the bar, and, for such a big conversation, they *had* to have dinner together. Plus, Mary rationalized that if they didn't want the bar anymore, it all but proved they'd stolen the stories and burned them, just like Carole said in her letter.

Joanna invited everybody over to their house for a big pot roast dinner after her dad let slip that the bar might be up for grabs. Once they were all welcomed into the house and seated for dinner, Judd and Fred got right to business. They spoke about, in general terms, what the bar might sell for, what the taxes were like, how much the value had gone up since renovating, and so on while they ate.

Mary listened uninterestedly as they spoke and curiously looked at the decorations on the wall. She couldn't help but feel like a stranger in her daughter's home.

"So, where is Carole these days?" Mary asked politely as Joanna passed her a bowl of green beans.

"Oh, she's in school now. Remember?" Joanna said offhandedly.

"No, I didn't know that. I hadn't heard anything. What school?" Mary asked.

"Just a little community college around the home she went to." Joanna took a bite of her dinner and nodded as if to signal that the conversation had reached its end. But Mary saw through this and did her best to keep her feigned interest up.

"That's great! Will she be visiting over the holidays or anything?"

"Not sure," Joanna said shortly.

"Oh, okay. Well, would you tell her the next time you talk to her that we'd love to hear from her, too?"

Joanna squinted slightly at her mother at this question as if she was trying to figure out if the interest in Carole was innocent or not. "Well…" she finally said hesitantly, and Fred looked over at her as if on cue.

"We don't know where Carole is," he said flatly. "Just tell them. She was trouble when she lived here, and now she's off causing trouble somewhere else."

"So, she isn't in college?" Mary asked sharply.

"Well, she was on the roster when we called," Joanna offered. "But she didn't sign up with an address or a phone number or anything, so that's all we know."

The rest of the dinner passed tensely. Fred decided against buying the bar, which did nothing to help Mary's anger toward her daughter and son-in-law. Nothing more was said about Carole.

* * *

Fifteen years later, Mary and Judd had both passed away, leaving Garrett the sole heir to a large farm and the bar, which was thriving. Between managing both, he didn't have time for much else and never married. It was then that one last letter from Carole arrived in the mail.

Garrett knew better than to pass it on to Joanna and Fred. A few years back, they'd gone looking for Carole, and while they didn't find her, they did find ample evidence that she'd been in trouble—real trouble like jail and a schizophrenia diagnosis. For them, any hallucination at all was a clear sign of demonic presence. They were devastated, and the mention of her name since then was just shy of being explicitly forbidden. Garrett opened the letter, unaware that it would be the last time he ever heard from his niece.

Grandma Mary,

I know it's inexcusable how long it's been since I've written. I miss you terribly. I want to visit soon, but I am quite poor. Since I last wrote, quite a bit has happened. I was diagnosed with paranoid schizophrenia a couple of years after Rose was born. I now live on Social Security and can regularly take medication. It's helped quite a bit. I struggled for several years with substance abuse and homelessness but am now clean and living with my boyfriend. He also has schizophrenia, so we are able to help each other, but sometimes it is hard. He struggles with different things than I do. But I am happy to help. I am proud of my progress.

After so many address changes, I haven't received updates on my daughter in quite some time, but I will write her and her family a long-overdue letter, which I'll mail along with yours. She'll be sixteen next month. I plan on sending her Rose's locket since she is the last Rose in the family. I would also like to have the family stories you wrote to share with her when she turns eighteen. Could you send them to this address?

Tell everybody hello!

Love,
Carole

Garrett sent a short letter back telling her that, unfortunately, both her grandparents had passed and that the stories had been stolen, possibly burned. He wished her well and told her to reach out if she ever needed anything. But she never wrote back.

And with Carole's last letter and the years of silence that followed, the well-storied matriarchal family tree that began with the appearance of a Rose finally came to an end almost as mysteriously as it began: with the disappearance of a Rose. The family stories had been burned, and the last daughter who'd inherited the locket never returned. Nobody ever knew whether Carole, like her ancestors before her, met fairies or dragons to guide her on her way, though her parents claimed she'd been overtaken by demons. Despite whatever happened to her before she finally disappeared forever, she did manage to send the locket that had survived so many generations of women in the mail. She hoped that it would reach the last little Rose—wherever she was in the great wide world—so that maybe she would know, at the very least, that her mother loved her, even if the rest of the family's stories had been lost.

PART 3

MY BEGINNING

CHAPTER 21

THE CRASH

When I finally closed my second notebook, I felt dazed from the explosion of writing. It occurred to me that it might be worth combining the documentation of my own experiences from the past few months with the strange and winding story I'd just composed. The whole plotline felt like a desperate attempt to make sense of everything but didn't quite seem complete yet. It was while I was busy compiling the writings from my notebooks—both fiction and fact—in some semblance of order that my mom interrupted.

She knocked on my door just before lunch and carefully walked into my abhorrently messy room. This was something that hadn't happened in several years. I had spent most of my adolescence shoving both my parents out of my room until they finally quit coming in.

"Hey, Mom," I said curiously as I looked up from my notebook. She had been acting strange since I'd come home, and I wasn't sure what to make of it. She sat down on the bed next to me.

"Hey, Iz," she said. "I just thought I'd come in and check on you."

"Oh? You're not here to tell me to clean my room or sign up for college, are you?" I asked sarcastically.

She smiled nervously at me. My birthday had been such a heated event, but it was followed by a strange sort of defeat that I had never seen before from her. She'd always been fierce about her opinions on my behavior, and the lack of that lately didn't make any sense to me.

"No, I just… I know that the past couple of months have been a little hard on you, and I just wanted to let you know that…" She trailed off and looked around my room. "I'm sorry for the way we handled the information about your adoption."

I didn't know what to say. I froze. She finally turned back to look at me, a nervous smile anticipating a response.

"You are?" I asked, incredulous.

"I think that if we had told you sooner, you might not have felt the need to run off and go looking for answers yourself," she said. "When you told us you were going, I knew we had to let you."

"You did?" I was bewildered.

"I didn't like it. I hate that you ran off with Matt and that you didn't call. But I knew you were already upset with us. Whether I like it or not, you've always learned things the hard way, and…" She shrugged. "After being your mom for this long, I've learned that no matter what I do, you're going to do what you want."

I gave an uneasy laugh at this but continued to look at her like an alien who'd descended onto my planet unexpectedly.

"Thanks for saying that, Mom," I said. I closed my notebook in my hands nervously. "I'm sorry, too. I know I'm hell on wheels. I just—"

She waited for me to finish my thought, but it had been so long since we'd spoken like this, the whole thing felt foreign. We were much better at arguing about what I wore or why my behavior was unacceptable.

"I'm not like you or Dad," I said, looking up at her face to see if this had upset her, but she was listening calmly, "and now that I've learned more about Carole, I don't think I'm like her either."

My mom moved closer to me on the bed until we sat shoulder to shoulder, both leaning up against the pillows. It reminded me of the way we used to lay in my bed together every night and read books.

"I know," she said, wryly. "I wanted to tell you 'I told you so.'"

"I knew it!" I interjected.

She gave a little exasperated chuckle. "Yes, well, I wanted to, but I held back because I knew it would upset you, and I feel like…" She paused. "I've done enough of that this year."

"Well, thanks, Mom," I said and put my head on her shoulder. She wrapped her arm around me.

"Even if you had to find out the hard way, I always knew you weren't like Carole. For a long time, I didn't like that you weren't like me either, that you refused to adhere to the rules and expectations we set. But you've always been your own person, Iz. It took me until this year to see it, and I'm sorry."

"It's hard to be my own person," I said softly.

"Yes," she said. "But if anyone can do it, it's you."

We sat there on my bed together as I let this sink in. I hadn't realized until this moment what a jerk I'd been to my parents, how selfishly I'd been acting, and how much I missed the smell of my mom's hair.

"I, um. I know you probably don't want me to read it, but can I ask what you're writing about?"

"It's a book," I said, lifting my head off her shoulder. "I decided to write a book about all of this. I don't know if it's going to be any good, but I don't know how else to get out how I feel."

She nodded and looked around my room again. Whether she was planning on how to clean it once I moved out or if she was genuinely curious about the one room in the house she'd avoided for years, I couldn't tell. I watched as her eyes wandered over the walls and the floor.

"Maybe I'll let you read it," I said, despite feeling dread rise in my belly as this comment came out of my mouth, "but only if you keep acting weirdly nice."

She laughed. "Moms aren't supposed to be nice all the time."

"Well, I had to ask, at least," I said, my tone closer to my normal, sarcastic tease.

She got up from the bed and stood in the middle of my room. "You *do* need to clean your room, Izzie," she said with a disapproving look, then followed it up with an awkward smile. "But if you need to write a book, then write a book. I'll be in the living room if you need me."

"Okay," I said, unsure how to respond. She carefully stepped over the clutter on my floor and closed the door behind her. I was left to wonder how it was that I had been such a self-absorbed jerk yet been rewarded with such grace.

* * *

A few weeks after this encounter with my mom, with the end of my book in sight, I woke up one morning and immediately felt sick. I ran to the bathroom and threw up in between tears. My breasts ached the way they sometimes did before a particularly heavy period, but the half-moon had come and gone in the last week, and there I was, barfing first thing and with sore breasts. Pissed beyond reason that I'd somehow fallen so deep into my writing that I'd missed my period and not noticed, I cried in the bathroom until I heaved and hiccupped.

Finally, I put myself in the shower, got dressed, and headed to the store. The first thing I needed to do was make sure this was actually happening.

I thought about calling Matt. We'd had a couple of scares before, and I'd always told him then. But as much as I wanted to, I just couldn't. Things had been weird ever since we got back from the road trip, and most of the weirdness had probably been my fault.

I'd been sitting with a strange kind of guilt; maybe I'd been wrong to get so upset with Matt. Especially after my mom had unexpectedly apologized to me, I felt as though maybe Matt also deserved an apology for being dragged through my emotional turmoil and then, immediately afterward, put on the back burner. Though we'd talked a bit, a nervous distance between us materialized that had never been there before. Then again, I told him I needed to write desperately. We'd made it the last month and a half of the school semester without much contact, so I figured surely he understood. And if not, was it so wrong to put him through exactly what he'd put me through?

I bought the pregnancy test and stopped by the gas station to get a drink and hang out. I figured I'd just wait with one of the sticks in my pocket, drink until I couldn't drink anymore, and find out my results in the gas station bathroom.

Halfway through the largest size soda money could buy, Matt walked in the door.

"Hey," he called out to me.

"Hey, yourself." I hugged him and found that he was happy to return it. Maybe we weren't so bad after all. He kissed me on the forehead.

"What are you doing up here? I haven't seen you out in civilization in forever." He laughed. "Does this mean you're finished with your book?"

I did my best to smile back at him. "I'm getting really close, but I think I'm gonna take a break for a while. I know what parts I still need to write and everything, but I can't keep on writing day and night like this. It's making me kind of crazy."

"Well, that's good. I think maybe a slower pace could be okay. And if you know where it's going, there's no hurry."

"Yeah," I said happily, feeling better and better by the moment. Maybe telling him the truth wouldn't be so hard after all.

"I know I've been pestering you like crazy lately but, uh, do you want to do something today? I've got a friend coming in later, but I'm free until about five," he offered.

"Oh. Who's coming in? I'd like to hang out." But as I finished that sentence, my stomach took a nasty turn. The liquid I'd been inhaling was ready to pronounce me pregnant or sick; I made a face. "Um, hold on. Don't leave. I'll be right back." I dashed off toward the bathroom.

After conducting my private science experiment, I washed my hands and capped the test. Sadly, I wouldn't know the answer until later. I could hardly stay in the bathroom the full five minutes needed to see a result. I didn't want to give Matt any reason to suspect anything. Not yet, anyway.

I came back out to find Matt standing where I'd left him.

"Sorry." I gave him a cheesy grin.

"You alright?" he asked.

"Yeah," I said but left it at that. I wanted to tell him that I'd woken up sick and my whole chest felt heavy. That I'd completely missed my period, and I wanted him to help me make the kinds of plans we always made when I might be pregnant. But I held my tongue. I didn't know how to come back to him in the same casual way he'd come back to me when he'd arrived home and dragged me out to the lake. I felt awkward—the same kind of awkward my mom must have felt when she came into my room to apologize. That, and I had the sickening feeling that this time wasn't a scare. It wouldn't be just my life and Matt's that I might be ruining.

"I don't know about you, but I kind of planned on eating junk today and watching a bunch of TV. You in?" he asked.

"That sounds perfect." I smiled. And it did. I needed a fat person's portion of chocolate ice cream as soon as possible.

We wandered around the gas station collecting as much junk as we could carry to the register, then I followed him back to his house. Without looking at the results, I hid the pee stick in the console of my car on the drive over.

I didn't know how to begin my apology to Matt, but once we'd settled in on the couch with all our junk food and piles of blankets, I reached for his hand and said, "Hey. I don't know how to say this, but I'm really sorry."

"What?"

"Yeah, I just feel like maybe I've been being a jerk for the past few months because I've been trying to figure all this stuff out. I shouldn't have been mad at you for wondering what I'm doing in the fall. It's a good question. And I'm sorry I fell headfirst into writing a book and abandoned you for half the summer after you helped me go looking for answers."

His ears were turning pink. He waved his hand. "No, I know. Don't worry about it. I know these past few months have been weird. It's fine."

"Are you sure?"

"Yeah," he said as his cheeks tinged even pinker. He leaned over and kissed me.

Though I didn't understand why he was so quick to brush everything off, I was glad to have it off my chest. Next, I had to figure out how to tell him about the pregnancy test. But I didn't feel like jumping our relationship straight back into overdrive right away. I didn't say anything to him right then, but I could hardly think about anything else.

We sat on the couch all day stuffing our faces, kissing during commercials, and running increasingly stupid commentary on the shows we watched. Though it felt a little awkward to be back in his arms, I felt as though things would fix themselves, given enough time. And for the first time since I'd graduated, I finally had the thought that it was time for me to decide where I would go in the fall and consider how that would affect my relationship with Matt.

The only thing that I couldn't get off my mind—couldn't write off—was the worry that, if schizophrenia did indeed pass down maternally, was I tempting fate with a life not my own? Though I'd worried all summer about whether *I* might turn over to the sickness in a few years, cursing an innocent child was a fear greater than any I'd felt. Somewhere in the back of my mind, I knew the disorder wasn't as magical as seeing unicorns or predicting the future. But since Matt didn't yet know that I might be pregnant, I kept this worry locked behind my teeth when we kissed.

A little before five, he started getting antsy and said that my parents probably wanted me home. I gave him a weird look, but then remembered that his friend was coming in.

"Who did you say your friend was?" I asked.

"Oh. It's one of my bros from school. He's actually headed to Kansas but thought he'd spend a night here on the way and catch up."

"Okay, cool. Well, let's do lunch tomorrow?" I kissed him on the cheek.

"Sure, that would be good."

The moment I got in my car, I dug in the console for the pregnancy test. When I finally mustered the courage to look at the tiny little screen, my heart skipped a beat. *Positive.*

I hadn't even started the car before starting to cry. Like a flood, sobs fell out of me in drenching waves of violence. I suddenly felt like Melody when she knew she was pregnant but hadn't yet told her parents. I turned the key and looked back up at the house. Matt wasn't near the window so, luckily, I'd be able to sneak off without him knowing. Putting the car into drive, I pulled away from the curb and made my way to the only place I knew to go.

I called my sister.

"Hey, Ronnie, I'm staying out late tonight. Can you let Mom know?"

"Yup," she said. "Where are you going?"

"The lake."

When I got to the lake, I decided to follow the path that had previously burned me—the spot where the cop had plucked me out of the tree when I'd run off to find quiet away from my family. Near that path, not as far out as I'd gone last time, was a little clearing just big enough for two sleeping bags. It was where Matt and I had claimed each other's virginities. I thought it made sense to go back there and think about what to do next.

Though I didn't have a sleeping bag or even a blanket to lay out, I did have a towel in my car. I parked under a different set of trees, a place I was sure my car wouldn't be found, and hiked out toward the spot, towel in hand. The sun was still out so, still crying, I decided to strip down and go for a little swim.

Though my stomach felt strange and my breasts bobbed with an almost renewed buoyancy, being in the water calmed me. As the sun began to fall behind the trees, I got out and soaked up as much of the dying light as I could to dry off and warm up.

Though I thought about returning home, I decided to stay. After all, I wasn't ready to look anybody in the eye. I had a feeling that anybody who knew me well enough would immediately know something was wrong.

As twilight turned into evening and the fireflies came out to glitter, I tried to plan how I would tell Matt about our predicament the next day. At the very least, I thought dryly, I knew where I'd go in the fall.

I'd go live in his little apartment with him. I'd hold off on school, though. No point enrolling while pregnant and without a clue as to what career to pursue. I'd get a job, though. Any old job would do.

It wasn't worth mulling over how Matt would react to all this. We'd been together over five years at this point. We'd been through the planning. Everything was up to me. He'd always promised to leave it up to me.

It wasn't Matt that I was worried about. It was my parents. I would wait to tell them until after I'd told Matt and we'd figured out a plan. We'd tell his parents first. Though we hadn't ever approached them during previous scares, they were more open about these sorts of things. I'd always hoped that they'd help with the planning. That meant that tomorrow night at dinner, Matt would have to come over and sit through the painful explanation to my parents with me.

I already knew how my parents would react, though. There wasn't much I could plan for except building up the courage to sit through the inevitably uncomfortable conversation. My mom would cry, and my dad would pepper us with as many grim questions as he could think of. There would be a ton of pressure from them both to get married, keep the baby, do the right thing. Not that those things were outside of what I thought Matt and I would probably do—but it doesn't help to be pressured into things like that.

The night wore on, and I watched the stars begin to move above me as I lay on my towel. Suddenly, I heard a car nearby. I sat up to look around, then heard two car doors slam shut and the distant murmur of voices laughing and earth crunching beneath shoes.

I lay back down on my towel. Cops didn't laugh. It was probably just some kids coming out to drink or find a quiet place in the woods to get naked. I didn't really care.

I tried to move my thoughts to buying maternity clothes or packing up to move in with Matt or buying items for a baby like a crib and bottles and onesies. But I couldn't get anywhere beyond telling Matt and our parents. I didn't know what would happen after that. The only thing that occurred to me was that I would have to go to the doctor soon.

I was off the footpath near the water and lying flat on the ground, so as long as they didn't come to this exact spot, they'd probably walk right past me.

But as the footsteps got closer, I heard a voice say, "It's over here. You're going to love this spot."

My breath caught in my throat.

Why was Matt out here?

Like lightning, I jumped up, grabbed my towel, and hid behind a tree. Sure enough, Matt and a petite brunette girl walked straight into the spot where I'd just been contemplating my new life.

"Did you hear something?" the girl asked. I froze.

"Nah, baby. That's just the sounds of the forest. Come on, let's lay these blankets down."

I watched in horror as they put blankets down on the exact spot my towel had been just moments before. I couldn't move. I was stuck. There wasn't a clear way back to the footpath except for the one they were now blocking. If I was to get away, I'd have to climb through the brush and would surely make a ruckus doing so.

I watched in horror as they lay down and began kissing before, finally, I couldn't take it anymore and leapt out from behind the tree in an attempt to dash past them.

Both of them screamed in surprise. "Sorry," I yelled between the tears running freely down my cheeks. "Don't mind me. I've just—" As I got to the footpath, I took off sprinting toward my car.

"Wait!" Matt called behind me.

The girl yelled at him, too. "Come back! Don't leave me out here!"

But I kept running as fast as my legs would take me. I had to get out of there. I couldn't think straight. I just ran and ran for my car. But before I could reach it, Matt caught up with me and tackled me to the ground.

"Don't!" I screamed. "Get off me!"

But he had a good hold on my ankle, and he refused to let go.

"Please, Izzie, please. I can explain," he gasped.

"No. I don't want your explanation. Let go of me! Let go!" I kicked violently until my ankle was set free.

I scrambled to my feet and he rushed after me again, this time pinning me up next to my car.

"Izzie, please. You have to understand," he begged.

I froze as he pushed my shoulders up against my car and looked him in the eyes.

"I already understand," I said coldly. "Are you going to let me go home or not?"

"Not," he said. "I didn't know what we were after the road trip. We had that big fight and I know we both apologized, but you quit coming to see me. You quit answering my phone calls. It was so long, and I didn't know."

"I don't want to hear your stupid excuses," I shot back and shoved him off.

He let go of my shoulders and stepped back. "I'm sorry. Please. Let me explain. We can fix this."

"Save it," I said and got in the car. He stepped back and let me drive off. In the rearview mirror, I saw the girl come walking out of the woods toward him as I left.

I cried the whole way home. The lake wasn't safe anymore. And if the lake wasn't safe, nowhere was.

CHAPTER 22

CONFESSIONS

———

The house was quiet by the time I got back. I let myself in through my bedroom window. But after looking around at my room and seeing all the evidence of Matt from the past five years, I went to my sister's room.

I tapped on the door as quietly as I could, then slowly opened it and peeked in. She was sitting in bed with a scrapbook and a pile of papers laid out in front of her when she looked up. Immediately, she knew something was wrong. My tear-streaked cheeks probably gave it away. She moved all her stuff onto the floor in a pile so I could sit down next to her.

"What happened?" she asked.

"I'm an idiot," I said. "I don't want to talk about it. I just need a hug."

She hugged me. I tried to keep my tears in check, but instead of exploding out, they just burned my eyes and seared their way through tightly shut eyelids.

Once I found some control over my breath, I asked, "Why are you still up?"

She smiled mysteriously. "I've been doing a lot since your birthday," she said quietly. "I knew as soon as I saw it that Mom and Dad were probably going to hand me the same kind of paperwork they gave you. Or dump some new information in my lap. Or something equally as stupid." She grinned at me. "But I'm a step ahead of them."

"What?"

"I don't think Mom realized I was here when she got your paperwork out. I had come home for lunch to pick up a few things and heard her yelling about it from the kitchen. She was telling Dad how he really ought to clean out his half of the closet because getting to the paperwork they'd hidden there was really difficult."

Ronnie beamed at me. "Later that week, when the house was empty, I picked the closet clean. I found the folder with my name on it, and I've been putting everything of mine together in a scrapbook late at night after they go to bed."

"Oh, my God, Ronnie," I breathed. "Let me see." I smiled as she reached over the side of the bed to lift the stack of papers and scrapbook. Maybe our mom was right about the scrapbooking thing. It helped. Familiar paperwork looked up at me from the pages but with different names, dates, and photos attached.

"Dude, how have you been so quiet about this for so long?" I asked incredulously, paging through what she'd already arranged in the scrapbook.

She shrugged. "Yours was way more intense than mine. My birthmother seems, I don't know, a little closer to what I expected her to be. There weren't any big surprises in my folder that could compare to yours. I kind of figured you needed space to figure it out."

"Thanks," I said. "I've been hard at work on my own project, too, actually."

"Yeah? What is it?"

"I've been writing a book. It's just kind of about what happened to me with all this. And the things I wish I knew."

She nodded. "That's really cool. How far along in the story are you?"

I took a deep breath; my mind flashed back to the lake, then back to the pile of chapters I'd left in my room. Though Rose's fictional story had been wrapped up, the chapters of all the facts I'd learned on the road trip still hung in limbo. I had more to write before I could put a bow on all of it. But the day's events threatened the confidence I'd previously had about reaching some kind of epiphany about how to conclude the story.

"Pretty close to the end, I think," I finally said. "That, or close to a new beginning."

"I like when stories end with new beginnings."

"Yeah. Me too."

We sat on the bed for a moment, both lost in the cogs of our thoughts. Ronnie began working on her scrapbooking again. Though I sat perfectly still on her bed as she taped and arranged, I could still feel my heart racing, my stomach turning somersaults, my hands shaking. I couldn't see anything in my mind's eye except the two pink lines of that pregnancy test and the desperation in Matt's eyes after chasing me to the car. It didn't feel real, but I had to tell somebody.

"I want you to know something before Mom and Dad do," I said suddenly. She looked up at me in alarm and, before I lost my nerve, I spit out the news. "Today I found out I'm pregnant and that Matt has been cheating on me."

Her mouth dropped open.

"Yeah," I whispered, fearing my voice would crack again under all the pressure. "Tomorrow is going to be a big day."

"A very big day," she said, eyes alive with worry. "What are you going to do?"

I smiled weakly. "Well, I guess I have to tell Matt."

She nodded at me. "I'll be here when you tell Mom and Dad."

"Thanks. I'm going to go to bed now, I think I've calmed down enough to have a chance at falling asleep." I glanced at the clock. It was almost one in the morning. I still had time to get a good night's rest. I'd certainly need the energy in the morning.

* * *

When I woke up, the house was empty. I rolled over to bask in the comfort of sleeping in at my parents' house. It wouldn't be long before I'd be out somewhere in the world on my own. I touched my belly. I couldn't tell if there was anything in there, but I tried to imagine it again. It was like trying to daydream something into existence.

Before I told my parents, I needed to talk to Matt. Though I thought long and hard about keeping the pregnancy a secret to spite him, I knew it wouldn't work. Gossip got around in this town, and it wouldn't be long before he came to find me after he heard.

I got up, showered, and got dressed before looking at myself hard in the mirror. *You can do this. You're going to listen, and then you're going to leave.* But I couldn't tell if the girl in the mirror was paying attention or not. Then I got in my car, put her in drive, and hit the first speed dial on my phone.

"Izzie?" He picked up before I'd made it out of the neighborhood.

"Hey, Matt," I said.

"Hey, I just—"

"Don't worry about it. Can you meet me for brunch right now? Are you free?"

"What? Yeah, I mean, I need to put on some pants real quick—"

"Okay," I cut him off. "Meet me downtown. We need to have a really big talk."

Before he could respond, I hung up.

I took the long way around the loop to downtown. I didn't really care if he had to wait for me to arrive. As I drove, I tried my best to rehearse what to say to him. I could barely keep my thoughts straight.

When I finally pulled up, he was waiting on the bench outside. He was wringing his hands and jiggling his leg. I nodded to him and, for a moment, felt like a cowboy acknowledging—as polite as he could—a man he planned to duel with in the streets later that day. I watched Matt get up and stumble toward my car door to open it. I felt as nervous as he looked, but he didn't know the half of what this talk would be about.

We sat down and waved at the girl behind the counter, who gave us a grin and a thumbs up. That's one of the things about small-town restaurants. The folks know you and what you like.

After sitting in awkward silence for a few minutes, I said, "Listen. I'll let you tell me everything once, so this is your chance. I don't ever want to hear any of this again. Please tell me the truth."

I did my best to keep a straight face, keep my tears in, and stay in control of my throat's wobbliness. My whole body felt stiff from how much energy it took to hold myself still.

He squirmed in his seat and gazed off into the distance for a moment before finally speaking.

"It started at the New Year's party I went to with a bunch of my friends. I knew her from class, but we all got really trashed and that night was the first time I made a mistake. We slept together that night."

He actively avoided my eyes. I had some kind of incredulous fascination with the sudden knowledge that I'd completely missed an entire train wreck.

"After that, there were other times. She tried to get me to call her my girlfriend, but I wouldn't. We kind of just ended up being friends with benefits. She knew about you from the beginning, but it didn't stop her. Or me." He shifted uncomfortably in his chair. "I tried to tell you last night. It's not an excuse. I know I've fucked up. It's just that I didn't know what to do without you near me. I hated being on the phone with you because it made me miss you more. The letters you wrote me, the emails you sent, it wasn't enough. Or maybe it was too much. You're a writer, and there's no way I'd ever be able to write anything half as beautiful as what you'd written me. What was the point?"

He paused to take a deep breath. Tears were welling up in his eyes, and he tipped his head upward in an attempt to keep them from falling down his cheeks.

"Are you telling me that you left me in the lurch all that time because you didn't think the letters or emails you wrote would be good enough? You didn't call because you couldn't bear to miss me?" I asked, incredulous.

He twisted his hands in his lap. "I know it sounds stupid. I just wanted to come home, and I couldn't. I don't think you'll believe me when I say this, but I'm going to say it anyway. That girl was just filling the hole where you used to be. I meant to tell you about it, to apologize and everything, for the times I'd messed up. But the time was never right. You've been in this funk since your birthday. I didn't want to be the tipping point that pushed you over the edge."

I raised my eyebrows at this, but kept my mouth shut. I was still in disbelief that he'd let so much time pass without saying anything about this to me. I knew that for the truth to come out in full, I needed to wait silently. It's always driven him nuts, the silent staring. It made his truth gush out.

"And I really thought that after being home, it would all go away. Even if I didn't tell you, being back home with you made it feel like it didn't happen, that I didn't mess anything up. Even though things felt weird because of all your adoption stuff, I don't know. It felt like something we could handle together?"

I was beginning to feel queasy. He shook his head and spoke down to the table.

"And then right after we got home from the road trip, we had that stupid fight over lunch and you quit answering the phone, quit coming out to see me. You kept giving me the book excuse. I genuinely thought we were done."

It took all my self-control not to yell at him that I had, in fact, been busy writing a book. But I let him continue. I could feel my cheeks turning red despite my best efforts to hold in my rage.

"So that's why I went back to her, why I asked her to come visit. I thought you were done with me. If it helps, when we got to hang out after seeing each other at the gas station in the morning, I felt absolutely miserably guilty the whole day."

When he finally raised his head to look at me, I saw he hadn't been successful in holding in his tears. One had fallen down his cheek. His eyes were shining, the rest of the tears puddled at the bottom of his glass-green eyes.

"If you let me make this right, I will," he said, "but I understand if you don't want anything to do with me anymore."

We sat in silence again until the food arrived. I did my best to eat as much as I could despite a strong urge to run to the bathroom and throw everything up.

By the time he'd made it halfway through his plate, I finally said in a trembling voice, "I don't know what to think of all that. It's just a collection of horrible excuses. It sucked to find out the way I did, but now I guess I need to tell you why I was out there in our spot last night."

I could tell he hadn't been expecting any kind of explanation from me from the way he sat up extra straight.

"I took a test yesterday," I said quietly. "At the gas station when I ran off to the bathroom. I was there drinking as much as I could to pee on a stick."

His eyes widened in horror.

"I'm pregnant, Matt."

"What? I... you..." he stammered.

"After leaving your house, I went to our spot out at the lake to figure out how to tell you. I was worried all the stuff with my adoption had made things weird between us. When I apologized to you yesterday, I meant it. I know that I've not been myself, and I haven't been paying attention to you, but... just so you know, I've never strayed. When I told you I was writing a book, I was telling the truth. I feel like I have to write *something* to fill up this empty hole inside me. We didn't find Carole, and I don't know what I'm supposed to be doing."

Another tear fell down his cheek. I could feel my throat beginning to constrict, but I did my best to swallow the pain, keep my voice steady. "Anyway, I told you I'd call you when I figured out what I'd be doing in the fall, so I'm letting you know now. I still don't know much, but I do know I'm getting out of this town and will probably go get a job. If I do decide to have the baby, which I'm still not sure about, you don't have to be involved if you don't want to."

At this, he pushed his plate aside and slumped over the table, head in his arms. His shoulders began shaking.

I didn't know what to do or how to feel. I reached for my wallet and pulled out money to pay for our food. I stood and delivered it to the cashier by the door. When I got back to the table, he was in the same position, so I put my hand on his shoulder and bent over to whisper to him.

"Come on," I said softly. "We can have the rest of this conversation somewhere else."

He got up and followed me quietly out of the restaurant to my car. I pulled out of the parking lot and set out on the classic loop route. He stared out the window trying to hide his sobs, and I reached over and patted his leg awkwardly.

"Are you okay?" I asked. My eyes were beginning to flood with tears, making it hard to drive.

"I should be asking you that," he said in a small voice.

I snapped and started crying. A restaurant was one thing. My car was another. Big sobs started shaking my body until I had to pull over on the side of the road. I threw the car in park, jumped out, and ran to the ditch just as what little food I'd eaten came back up. I puked and heaved and sobbed until there was nothing left to throw up. Matt appeared by my side at some point to hold back my hair and rub my back, which made me sob even harder.

I got back into the car and sat helplessly behind the steering wheel. I opened a mint from the local drive-in and put it in my mouth. It didn't make me feel any calmer.

"To answer your question," I said between hiccups, "no, I am not okay. Not at all."

He started sobbing again in the passenger seat next to me. "Me neither."

I finally asked him, "What do we do? What should I do?"

He shook his head, and I gave up. Incensed with him, terrified—it didn't matter. Crawling over the center console,

I curled up into his lap and cried until I couldn't cry anymore. I didn't know what else to do. There was no one in the world I knew better, and yet I felt as though I was sitting in the lap of a stranger.

"Did you love her?" I asked.

"No," he said. "I liked to have her around to fill up the empty space where you were supposed to be."

"You know that makes it worse."

"I know."

I put my head back on his shoulder to mull this over. He was warm.

"Are you going to keep the baby?" he asked.

"I don't know. I thought this would go differently. I thought we would do it together, but…"

"But then you found out I was a lying, cheating asshole?"

"Pretty much."

"Well. I'm willing to help you in whatever way you need."

"I don't know…" I hiccupped. "I don't know what to do."

"Do you hate me?" he asked.

"Right now, yes. Do you hate me?"

He laughed. "No. I can't live without you, and I was a fool to have tried. Look how selfish I've been. Right when you needed me, I screwed it all up."

I laughed. "Yeah, you fucked up big time."

He began laughing with me. Soon we were laughing like hyenas in the passenger seat of my car.

"I hate you, I hate you." I laughed until my belly ached. I laughed until I began crying again and, bewildered by the clear lack of control over my emotions, I crawled back over to the driver's seat and desperately tried to take deep breaths. Then I realized I had something to sober us both up.

Reaching into the center console, I pulled out the pregnancy test. It still read positive. When I handed it to him, he held it like gold, frozen and unable to react to the truth in his hands.

"There it is," I said. "A year ago, I would have known exactly what to do with a test like that."

"A year ago," he repeated softly.

I put the car in drive and pulled back on the highway. My sister's comment came back to mind. Maybe if I drove, I'd feel like this conversation could go somewhere. At the very least, a drive wouldn't last forever. Every drive has to stop somewhere.

"What's your book about?" he asked. "You still haven't told me."

"Everything that's happened to me since my birthday and…" I paused. "Everything I wished had happened before, I guess. Some of it's true, some of it's pretend."

"Am I in your book?"

"Yep."

"Oh," he said. "Have you finished it?"

I turned onto the road that would lead us back to his truck downtown. The question was the same as my sister's but hearing it from his mouth jolted me into the reality of my situation. I knew how the story had to end, at least when it came to Matt. I looked at myself in the rearview mirror to remind myself of what that determined girl in the mirror had told me earlier that morning.

"I'm almost done," I responded softly. "There's just a few things left to write."

I drove down Main Street and pulled into the restaurant parking lot. I parked next to his truck but didn't unbuckle or move to get out.

"I'm glad we had this talk," I said, unlocking the doors.

"Is this it?" he asked. "Are we over? We didn't figure anything out. What's going to happen?" There was slight panic in his voice.

"I figured it out," I said.

"Were you planning on filling me in?"

"I thought it was obvious, Matt," I finally said. "I can't do this with you anymore. I'm done."

"What about the baby?"

"Forget about it," I said and pointed to his truck.

"But, Iz, I—"

"You told me everything, right?"

"Yeah, but—"

"That's all I needed to hear. You can get out now."

He looked at me blankly then reached for the door. "I just want you to know that I'm sorry," he said and got out.

I blinked back more tears and squeezed the steering wheel until he closed the door. I didn't wait to see him get in his truck. I just drove home.

CHAPTER 23

THE LAST ROSE

———

I drove back home with a heavy heart to waste away the afternoon hiding in my room, working up the courage to tell my parents the truth over dinner. It wasn't something I looked forward to. I somehow knew exactly what they would say yet feared how they would say it—feared that this would be the final straw and they'd be done with me and my nonsense once and for all.

I hated that I would ruin what had been a magical moment between my mom and me. She had just turned the corner toward loving me as the unique individual I was, accepting that I needed more freedom, but all that would soon dissipate. I knew she would call this thing inside my belly carelessness. And I wasn't looking forward to seeing the deep, withering disappointment in my father's eyes, either.

As I crawled into my bed, I was hit with the overwhelming feeling that I didn't feel anchored anywhere. Though I'd felt this kind of vast loneliness before, its urgency in that moment spooked me. I wondered what would happen if I were to vanish, to start over someplace new. Would they miss me? They didn't know anything about the version of me that lay dormant inside, waiting to find a place where I might belong.

Yes, they did their best to raise me to know the difference between right and wrong, but somewhere deep at the core of myself, I felt a tidal wave of panic threaten me with the soul-crushing promise of everlasting loneliness.

I was born alone to a mother I never called Mama, then taken home by strangers—wonderful people I could never seem to make proud. Someday I would die alone, too.

I thought that I would feel more adjusted after learning more about my birthmother. But the little snippets of her life that came out of the cracks were simultaneously overwhelming and severely lacking. I didn't feel like I belonged with the family I had *or* the family I'd lost. It was just me: floating along in this wild river without a raft to cling to. And with Matt gone, there would be another piece of my family gone forever. I couldn't bear to imagine how his parents would react to the double-whammy news of our breakup and the proof in my belly that we'd once loved each other.

But with the matter of our relationship settled, I felt strangely confident in how I would lay everything out for my parents. The instant I saw Matt kissing that girl out at the lake, I knew it was over. That wasn't something I would ever be able to simply move on from. I felt lucky that he had made it so cut-and-dried for me. And because it was clear that I had to walk away from him, it was clear that I would also walk away from the baby.

I'd spent the last month and a half writing my book at top speed, doing my best to fill in the unknown past of my family history with characters that felt almost too fictional when what I should have done was sit down and think about the future. That's what everybody wanted me to do. Somehow, the people around me knew better than I did where I had been, and they wanted to know where I would go, what I would do. But it just seemed to me that I was barreling into the future at top speed without a plan, without a map, and without a guide.

The past was fucked. My story had missing pieces. And as I lay in bed thumbing through the pages of my notebook, chapter by chapter, I wondered why I ever thought it would be a good idea to tell a story that would never be complete.

* * *

After we all sat down to dinner, Ronnie cocked her eyebrow at me from across the table. She wanted to know if I was going to tell our parents.

"Mom? Dad?" I asked tentatively. They glanced up. Ronnie was the only one with a good idea of what would go down, and her presence comforted me. I knew that if I needed her to, she would get in my car after dinner and listen to me cry as I drove around town in circles.

"What is it, Izzie?"

"I've got something to tell you," I said, staring at my plate. "I broke up with Matt today, and I'm pregnant."

The silence fell over us like the deathly quiet of a bomb's aftermath. I held my breath. When I looked up, both my parents were slack-jawed. My mom's mouth began to move wordlessly; my dad stared at me as if I'd suddenly turned purple. I cringed and waited for the worst.

"You... are you okay?" my dad finally asked.

"Pregnant?" my mom burst out. "Matt's? What happened?"

I just nodded. I didn't have the courage to tell them everything that had happened with Matt, and I felt dangerously close to tears. Or hysterical laughter. I experienced the same terrifying jolt of overwhelming emotion that had seized me in the car before I broke up with him. Either way, I dug my nails into my thighs in an attempt to keep it together. I waited for them to lay into me the way they always did. But nothing came. They didn't seem to know what to say. And for the second time since my eighteenth birthday, I saw an unfamiliar pair of people in front of me. They were older than I realized, tired and confused, yet their bewildered panic felt more alive than ever. I tried to think about how they must have felt as I told them in one short sentence how my life had taken two sudden and terrifying turns all in one day, but I couldn't fathom it.

"What are you... what are you going to do?" my mom asked. "I can't believe you, I—"

"Well," I cut her off, hoping to delay the lecture. My mind suddenly flashed back to the moment in the hotel, a moment where I'd had a supportive companion and hope for the future. "I haven't had a ton of time to parse through all of it, but I've been thinking that the baby has to go."

At this, my mom choked and violently burst into loud tears.

"I thought that I could give it up for adoption," I said quickly, talking over her. While I *had* considered the alternative, I decided that it simply wasn't something I could stomach. That, and I had no idea where to go, how much it would cost, and—correctly—assumed my parents would fully disown me if I made that choice.

My mom sniffled and took a deep shuddering breath. Her eyes were already red from the tears.

"Have you given more thought to your plans in the fall?" my dad asked. He had somehow returned to a logical state of mind, despite the chaos. "There's still time to sign up for school. You might have to take some time off to recover during a semester, but I'm sure your teachers would understand if you explained it to them."

"Yeah," I said. "I've been working on writing a book since I got back from the adoption agency." I paused. "I don't know if it's any good, but I think I would like to learn how to make it better."

"How will all the adoption stuff work out, though?" asked my mom.

"Well," I said. "Carole stayed at the facility until I was born, so maybe I could do that, too. And I could go to classes during the day."

"I'm sure you could probably work something like that out," my dad said. "We can call and check on all the details with the agency."

My mom got up from the table to blot her tears with a Kleenex. She returned to the table with paper and a pen. "First things first," she said, her voice shaking. "We need to get you to the doctor before you go anywhere. Do you know how far along you are?"

I squirmed in my chair.

"Well, Izzie?"

I winced apologetically, and she clicked her tongue.

"You didn't find your birthmother on that trip, but you decided to become one, is that it?"

I felt a wave of heat burn my face, and she angrily clicked her pen.

We stayed at the kitchen table well into the night, putting together the to-do list that would consume my next nine months. I stayed quiet as our parents discussed all the things I would need to do. Ronnie picked up the untouched plates in front of us and quietly did the dishes. I wondered how everything had gone so wrong so fast.

It was finally decided that, in September, when I would be four months pregnant, I'd leave for San Antonio to start my first semester at a community college and move in for my stay at the same agency I was adopted from.

* * *

The next two months passed in a disorienting blend of what felt like time staying frozen forever and taking sudden jumps forward. Though all four of us were unsure about how to talk about all the things that had happened in the past several months, we stumbled along through awkward talks about what to expect, God's wonderful plan for both me and my baby, and the never-ending list of things to take care of. I left my book unfinished at the time. It didn't seem relevant to muse over my own broken conception story when I was so busy worrying about starting the same kind of story all over again. I didn't yet know that the perfect ending lay just around the corner.

Not a week after I'd made the announcement to my parents, Matt's parents came over to the house and apologized profusely for what had happened with their son. They didn't like that I'd made the decision to give up the baby and asked if there was any way they could help raise the child. My mom shook her head at them politely but firmly. They both hugged me before they left and, when I looked out the window, I saw Matt sitting in the car waiting for them. I wanted to run outside and make him roll the window down, tell him to pinch me and wake me up from this awful dream where he'd cheated. But I fought the urge and instead watched as the car backed out of our driveway and left.

My mom accompanied me to all my doctor's appointments and made it her personal mission to make sure that I was taking my vitamins, eating properly, and following all the rules that I'd previously been unaware pregnancy came with. My belly began to swell up as did the fat in my cheeks, but it wasn't the physical changes that bothered me so much.

I mostly felt like I didn't have much of a choice about anything. I couldn't escape the crippling fear of being thrown into the world alone so soon when the plans I had for my future seemed feeble at best. Though I tried to rationalize that I was focusing on the future by choosing to attend community college, I couldn't shake the feeling that I hadn't yet found a place I belonged or a dream worth chasing. Truly, I began to wonder if any purpose in life existed for me at all. My mom did her best to remind me that, even though I was heartbroken, I needed to focus on happy thoughts.

"Your baby's temperament depends on it," she said. "Cheer up."

September arrived much too soon, so I began to clear out my room. It looked uncomfortably barren afterward. With Ronnie's help, I packed all the essentials for an extended stay at the adoption agency. Before I knew it, my car was stuffed full, and it was time to head off on my next adventure.

Before I left town, I had one last appointment at the doctor's office. My mom followed me in her car because, even though I would be leaving town after my appointment, she couldn't bear to miss it. I was beginning to think that she was somehow beginning to fall in love with the wiggly baby growing inside of me. That, or she felt powerful knowing that, because I was pregnant, I finally had to listen and follow her advice.

My mom smiled at me and held my hand as the technician took the ultrasound. I was uncomfortable and, frankly, annoyed at how much she'd hovered over me since I'd been pregnant. But I was also glad to know that somehow my pregnancy hadn't ruined the awkward love that had reemerged between us after I'd come home from the road trip.

I watched with terror and interest as the baby's head, fingers, and legs showed up on the screen. It no longer looked like a peanut the way it had at my last ultrasound. It was *definitely* a baby.

"If you want to, you can find out if your baby is a boy or girl today." The technician smiled. "I'll be right back with the printout."

"It's up to you," my mom said gently.

"I don't know." I hesitated. I felt uneasy thinking about the baby as a boy or a girl. It somehow felt more real. And as I thought about the kind of life I'd be giving to a baby who might grow up just as lost and alone as me, I began to feel sick.

"If you ask me, I'm pretty sure it's a girl," my mom said, as if we were sharing a juicy secret. I looked at her bright smile and couldn't help but feel my heart break a little, or maybe it was melting.

"Hey, Mom?" I asked. "Can I ask you something?"

"Sure," she said, leaning in.

"Are you going to be sad that you won't get to know your grandbaby?"

A strange look passed over her face, and she pulled her hand away from mine to run her fingers through her hair in thought. "Yes," she said, finally, "But I know God has a plan for you and this baby."

"You're not worried?"

"Worried about what?"

"I don't know. What it will be like for that baby to grow up without knowing us, how we'll feel knowing that out there somewhere is a little piece of me, or how I'm supposed to concentrate on school when I'm waddling around?" I closed my eyes and laid my head down against the back of the exam chair. Before my mom could formulate an answer, the technician reentered.

"So, what's the decision? Are you going to find out the gender?" she asked.

"Yes," I said suddenly.

My mom looked at me in surprise but reached out to accept the envelope from the technician.

"Whenever you're ready, the answer's in that envelope," the technician said and left again so that I could wipe the jelly off my belly and pull my shirt back down over my bump.

We left the doctor's office without saying a word to each other. I assumed that I'd startled my mom with my question and sudden interest in knowing the gender. She walked me to my car in the parking lot, hugging me before I got in.

"I know you're scared," she said, "but you'll be just fine." She handed me the envelope and patted my shoulder before turning to walk back toward her car.

It was finally time to go. I pulled out of the parking lot and headed toward the highway—the envelope still in my hand—and drove southbound to a future I didn't want. It didn't take long until I found myself pulling into the adoption agency parking lot for the second time.

* * *

I don't know how long I sat in my car in that stupid parking lot, staring at the front door of the Welcome Center. All I had to do was turn off the car, unbuckle, grab my duffel bag, and go in.

But I froze. It was as if all bodily functions had given out, yet my mind was running circles at top speed.

I had been in this same parking lot looking for my birth-mother just a few months ago. Matt had stolen information from the computer so casually. The lost months of my senior year now wandered through my thoughts. I felt guilty for trying to figure out if it was possible to find my birthmother, for thinking that by meeting her I might know more about the kind of person I might become. I thought about climbing in Matt's truck for a journey we'd started while still hungover after graduation night. And with the thought of Matt, I wondered incredulously how I'd completely missed when my boyfriend of five years fell away from me because I'd become so absorbed in finding and documenting some mystical family history.

I couldn't breathe for all the thoughts that rushed through my head while staring at the Welcome Center. I was about to put a baby through a life that would probably lead to the kind of empty desperation I felt when I first pulled into this parking lot. This child of mine—wiggly thing in my belly—would look for me. That's how these stupid stories always go. Kind of a shitty family tradition, right?

Then again, I wasn't prepared to be a mother. I'd just broken up with my boyfriend, I didn't know who I was, and I definitely didn't know what I wanted to be when I grew up. I also didn't have a job. With all my belongings in the trunk, I felt pretty close to homeless. There was nowhere I could run that this baby wouldn't follow me, and yet, I couldn't bring myself to get out of the car, live in a dorm with other pregnant women, and guarantee that this baby would find a home.

And what about a home for me? There wasn't a place in the world I could have gone that I would have felt welcome. I thought about getting out my cell phone and calling somebody. But the only person I could come up with was Matt, which made my heart ache, so I turned my attention to the envelope in my hand instead.

My mom's cheerful prediction that the baby was a girl rang in my ears, and though I'd held the envelope between my fingers nearly the whole drive down to San Antonio, I still hadn't opened it. I was terrified that she was right. The idea of a little girl melted my heart in all the scariest ways.

I watched helplessly as another car pulled into the parking lot and a young couple walked into the Welcome Center. Here to buy a baby, probably. I wondered what they would tell their child. I wanted to know if it was just my parents or if all adopted parents felt like their child, sometimes so foreign to them, was nevertheless a gift from God. But I was no object; I wasn't something that should have been wrapped up in a bow and delivered with a short warranty.

It didn't matter, though. They did their best. It was just that, for some reason, no matter how angry or how apathetic my thoughts became, I was trapped by my own cowardice in that stupid agency parking lot. I felt stuck in a circle that led to no answers.

Then, like an instant message from the divine, it dawned on me. None of this mattered. None of the things I was fretting about meant *anything*. I knew all I was going to know in that tiny zap of a moment, and a sudden rush of peace washed over me as I let it all go.

I got whiplash from how quickly I started digging in my duffel bag for my notebook and pen. I had to get my thoughts down.

I had given up on writing the last chapter of my book, the narrated version of my experience since April complete with some empty fantasy about who my ancestors could have been. But if I wanted to get to the end of the book, I had to make a decision. Right there in the parking lot that, five minutes before, had felt like a place of peril.

My heart raced at the possibility that I could save a story I once wrote off as broken and make it whole. Even better,

I could make two stories whole. And to do that, I had a big choice to make.

The questions about whether I'd give the baby away or keep it, go to school or get a job, become like my parents or my birthmother were all too specific—and they were weighing me down. I pushed them out of my head and wrote in my journal:

> *A wise computer once said that the answer to the question of the meaning of life was forty-two. But in fact, the meaning of life is invalid. There is no greater meaning; there is no before or after. I've walked to the edge and peered over. None of it matters. Plain and simple.*
>
> *The only problem is this little thing called awareness. We have too much of it. The fat and water and electricity that sloshes around in our heads is desperate for explanations. Desperate for stories. Desperate for structure. We are too stupid to comprehend absolute nothingness, so instead, we fill in the void with things we label with meaning.*
>
> *And yet, by labeling things with meaning, we enrich our lives. We give ourselves purpose. But only if we can label appropriately and with restraint.*
>
> *My past is only meaningful if I make it so. And the future is the same. I am not some predestined product, bound to any certain path or purpose. I'm a writer with a pen.*

And once I was done writing that strange little epiphany, I tossed the pen and notebook in the passenger seat and breathed a sigh of relief. I'd done it. I'd figured it out. It wasn't about finding some magical place full of people like me or desperately looking for someone else's path to follow. It didn't matter that I wasn't like my birthmother or my parents, and it didn't matter if I was. It didn't mean anything to leave behind a boyfriend not strong enough to live without me. My purpose in life wasn't out there somewhere. It was right in front of me. It was inside me. I was in charge of ascribing meaning or stripping it away. I was in charge of becoming my own person.

I looked down at the envelope in my hands and smiled. I was going to find out who my baby was. Carefully, I slit open the top of the envelope. After all, this seemed like the kind of thing that would be nice in a scrapbook.

I pulled out the soft black photo paper that had my name and the date at the top. I looked at the blurry black and white image of the baby growing inside me. As I closely examined the ultrasound, I found a little label on the photo that read: *Girl.*

Without thinking, I put my hand on my chest and fiddled with the golden heart-shaped locket. I hadn't taken it off since my birthday. But as I opened and closed it absentmindedly, beaming with excitement at both my revelation and the picture of my baby, I understood something else.

I had always felt alone without the stories of the family that came before me. It wasn't just that I had misplaced meaning on a history I would never know, didn't need to know; it was that I never thought about writing my *own* history, forging through the future and writing down the stories as they happened, and taking charge of the meaning around me as I named it.

It was time to forget about the things that didn't matter and focus on the ones who did. There was just one last chapter of the book I had to write, this one, and then my baby girl would be born. I would be in charge of navigating the stories we would write together, the life we would build. I would go to school and learn the art of writing, wait tables, apply for loans—whatever it would take to build a rich life with the only little human who would share both my blood and, more importantly, my stories.

I decided then, as I put the car in drive, that I would name her Rose for all the Roses who came before her, even if I was the only one. And anyway, I had a necklace to pass down.

As I pulled out of the parking lot and began to follow the roads back home, I thought of the way my mom smiled when she saw the ultrasound, the confidence in her voice when she said she believed that God had a plan for us despite knowing I'd long tired of that story, and the giddiness in her voice when she predicted that my baby was a girl. I wondered how she must have felt bringing Ronnie and me home from faraway hospitals, knowing that she would love us forever but also knowing that there'd be a tiny piece of us that would stay with the women we came from. I knew then why she had accompanied me to every doctor's appointment, every ultrasound: she'd never had that experience herself. And now, with my decision, the least I could do was ask for her help for the rest of the pregnancy, share that bit of magic with her. A fragile thing, yet somehow too, the most powerful thing I'd ever known was the love between mothers and daughters. It was up to me to mend that bond in preparation for creating a new one. I would have to learn how to become my own kind of mom soon enough.

But I would do these things on my own terms. After all, I wasn't quite like anybody else. I was my own person, and I liked it that way.

I called my mom when I reached the highway. I was nervous but excited to tell her of my plan, hoping like hell

276 · ROSE'S LOCKET

that she would welcome me back until I figured out how to stand on my own, knowing that while she'd probably feel exasperated, she might feel joyful, too.

"Hey, Mama, it's me," I said when she answered. "I have big news. I'm coming home. You're going to have a granddaughter."

ACKNOWLEDGMENTS

SPECIAL THANKS

Thank you.

To my parents, Glen and Joan Quist, who brought home more adventure than they bargained for, yet persisted with love and patience—and a whole ton of grit.

To all of my family members, the whole lot of you spread out from coast to coast, the ones closer to home, and the ones who have earned the honorary title of family. There is not enough space here to name each and every one of you, but I love you all.

To all of my friends who have endured phone calls and voicemails and announcements and ramblings about this whole process. You know who you are, and I am forever grateful for your love.

To Eric Koester, who found me on LinkedIn wondering where my writing would take me, then convinced me over a fifteen-minute phone call to join his authors' program.

To the amazing group of people at Creator Institute and New Degree Press including Margaret Danko, Brian Bies, Kristy Elam, Emily Price, Michelle Felich, and everyone else in this very special community of dreamers.

To the whole team of Alpha readers who read the first horrible draft of my book and somehow came back with compliments: Bradley Boucher, Megan Diaz, Brooke Hardy, Ryan Quist, Jenny Russell, Savannah Simmons, Daniel Stefanelli, and Kyle Vernor.

To the Beta readers who helped with all the final edits and offered their brutal honesty: Paula Ferguson, Danny Navarro, and Jenny Russell.

To my dear friend Josephine Davis for making such a beautiful map illustration for this book.

To Randy Skaggs for writing a perfect article about me and my book for *The Perryton Herald*.

But absolutely most of all—thank you, Emery. Thank you for cheering me on as I wrote my book, asking about whether there would be pictures and writing your own stories alongside me. Thank you for inspiring me to include all the fantastical creatures of your dreamworld into my own imagined family history. Thank you for being the first person I've ever met to be related to me by blood and showing me that life is about the moments we spend and the futures we build. It sometimes feels as though I can't pass on history that should be important to you about family, but I can pass on my name and my stories. So, Emery Rose, here is one of my stories. I love you more than you will ever know.

SUPPORT ACKNOWLEDGMENTS

To all of you who pre-ordered my book during the pre-launch campaign, participated in my Author Community, and walked with me through the exhilarating journey of writing and publishing my book—thank you for all your support. You helped me reach my goals, shared the exciting news, and cheered me on as I relentlessly chased one of my biggest lifelong goals: to write and publish a book! I couldn't have done this without help from all of you.

Thank you to: Aaron Beaver, Adrianne Court, Amahde Duncan, Amanda Missel, Amber Childress, Sally Anderson, Andrea Day, Andrew Clement, Angela Hardy, Anna Castanon, Anthony (AJ) Dvorak, Asha Hudson, Ashley Reyes, Barbara Johnson, Bert Bostic, Beth Headrick, Bethany Weston, Brandon Wayman, Bree Thiele, Dr. Brian Fehler, Brooke Hardy, Caitlen Juarez, Caitlyn Quist, Carla Sapoznikov, Charlene Simmons, Charles & Marimar McKeever, Cheryl Mann, Christie Smith, Colleen Gatewood, Courtney Mrsny, Crystal Iacuone, Danny Navarro, Deborah Finch, Desiree Thorpe, Diana Matuszak, Dmitriy Chernikov, Donna & Rex Mann, Ed Williamson, Eric Anders, Eric Koester, Felice Ferguson, Frances Wilm, Gabriel Miranda, Gina Vecchio, Ginger Meller, Greg Ferguson, Hannah Cunningham, Heather Koerner, Heidi Torres, Jaclynn Sapoznikov, Janet Slaughter, Jen Raebel, Jenny and Tyler Russell, Jeremy Stuart, Joan and Glen Quist, Jose Borunda, Kaitlyn Klattenhoff, Karen Freelove, Katie Doll, Kazi Sakiouzzaman, Kelly Barrett, Kelsey Smith, Kenny Jones, Kim Herring, Kyle Vernor, Laurie Quist, Leah Ferlita, Lori Lumley, Luis Gonzalez, Madeleine Dang, Mae Rock, Matt Devers, Meg McClain, Megan Diaz, Mary Huber, Melissa Rodriguez, Micha Czanik, Michelle Pustka, Michelle Simmons (both of you!), Michelle Perry, Mollie Ferguson, Monique Gautier, Paula Ferguson, Rebekah Leahey, Rhonda Appelhans, Rob Ruiz, Rosa Martinez, Russell Ferguson, Ruth Schoenhals, Ryan Quist, Salena Parker, Sam Cross, Sandi Vernor, Sandra Koerner, Sanlyn Ferguson, Sarah Collins, Savannah Simmons, Shannon Baughman, Shelby

Miller, Shota Yamaguchi, Stacy Kujawa, Stephanie Quist, Susan Lozano, Terri Martinez, Terry Peak, Tracy Ramacher, Tyson Harding, Vicki Gurley, Dr. Vivian Casper, Wanda Atchison, William Dyer III, Zane Simmons, and everyone who supported me anonymously.

APPENDIX

———

AUTHOR'S NOTE

Baxter, Cecilia, et al "Understanding Adoption: A Developmental Approach."
Paediatrics & Child Health 6, no. 5 (2001): 281-283.

Beach, Lee Roy. *The Psychology of Narrative Thought: How the Stories We Tell
Ourselves Shape Our Lives.* Bloomington, IN: Xlibris, 2010.

Erikson, Erik "The Life Cycle: Epigenesis of Identity." In *Identity: Youth and Crisis*,
91-140. New York: W. W. Norton, 1994.

Frankl, Victor E. *Man's Search for Meaning.* Boston: Beacon Press, 2006.

Hirsch, Marianne. "Family Pictures: Maus, Mourning, and Post Memory."
Discourse: Berkeley Journal for Theoretical Studies in Media and Culture 15, no. 2
(1992-93): 3-29.

Sansal, Boualem. *The German Mujahid.* Translated by Frank Wynne. New York:
Europa Editions, 2009.

Yehuda, Rachel, Nikolaos P. Daskalakis, Linda M. Bierer, Heather N. Bader, Torsten
Klengel, Florian Holsboer, and Elisabeth B. Binder. "Holocaust Exposure Induced
Intergenerational Effects on FKBP5 Methylation." *Biological Psychiatry* 80, no. 5
(2016): 372-80. https://10.1016/j.biopsych.2015.08.005/.

CPSIA information can be obtained
at www.ICGtesting.com
Printed in the USA
BVHW090853201220
595723BV00005B/12

9 781636 766300